Chesney—He wa~~...~~ ~~...~~ geance, and Keelock had ~~...~~

Neill—He had never killed a man, not even an Indian. Until the fighting started, he figured he was just along for the ride.

Cooley—He didn't give a damn about Keelock, all he wanted was the gold he had buried ten years ago at Mormon Cross.

Neerland—They'd hired him to hunt and kill Matt Keelock. He'd do that all right, but he was really fixing to get hold of Keelock's wife. He had some plans for that two-timing hussy that would curl the hair on a billiard ball.

THE KEY-LOCK MAN

BENDIGO SHAFTER
BORDEN CHANTRY
BOWDRIE
BOWDRIE'S LAW
BRIONNE
THE BROKEN GUN
BUCKSKIN RUN
THE BURNING HILLS
THE CALIFORNIOS
CALLAGHEN
CATLOW
CHANCY
THE CHEROKEE TRAIL
COMSTOCK LODE
CONAGHER
CROSSFIRE TRAIL
DARK CANYON
DOWN THE LONG HILLS
THE EMPTY LAND
FAIR BLOWS THE WIND
FALLON
THE FERGUSON RIFLE
THE FIRST FAST DRAW
FLINT
FRONTIER
GUNS OF THE TIMBERLANDS
HANGING WOMAN CREEK
HELLER WITH A GUN
THE HIGH GRADERS
HIGH LONESOME
THE HILLS OF HOMICIDE
HONDO
HOW THE WEST WAS WON
THE IRON MARSHAL
THE KEY-LOCK MAN
KID RODELO
KILKENNY
KILLOE
KILRONE
KIOWA TRAIL
LAW OF THE DESERT BORN
THE LONESOME GODS
THE MAN CALLED NOON
THE MAN FROM SKIBBEREEN
MATAGORDA
MILO TALON
THE MOUNTAIN VALLEY WAR
NORTH TO THE RAILS
OVER ON THE DRY SIDE
PASSIN' THROUGH
THE PROVING TRAIL

THE QUICK AND THE DEAD
RADIGAN
REILLY'S LUCK
THE RIDER OF LOST CREEK
RIVERS WEST
THE SHADOW RIDERS
SHALAKO
SHOWDOWN AT YELLOW
  BUTTE
SILVER CANYON
SITKA
SON OF A WANTED MAN
THE STRONG SHALL LIVE
TAGGART
TO TAME A LAND
TUCKER
UNDER THE SWEET-
  WATER RIM
UTAH BLAINE
THE WALKING DRUM
WAR PARTY
WESTWARD THE TIDE
WHERE THE LONG GRASS
  BLOWS
YONDERING

Sackett Titles by
Louis L'Amour

1. SACKETT'S LAND
2. TO THE FAR BLUE
   MOUNTAINS
3. THE DAYBREAKERS
4. SACKETT
5. LANDO
6. MOJAVE CROSSING
7. THE SACKETT BRAND
8. THE LONELY MEN
9. TREASURE MOUNTAIN
10. MUSTANG MAN
11. GALLOWAY
12. THE SKY-LINERS
13. THE MAN FROM THE
    BROKEN HILLS
14. RIDE THE DARK TRAIL
15. THE WARRIOR'S PATH
16. LONELY ON THE
    MOUNTAIN
17. RIDE THE RIVER
18. JUBAL SACKETT

LOUIS L'AMOUR
THE KEY-LOCK MAN

BANTAM BOOKS
TORONTO • NEW YORK • LONDON • SYDNEY • AUCKLAND

THE KEY-LOCK MAN

A Bantam Book / December 1965

2nd printing ..... June 1966	*6th printing ... October 1969*
3rd printing ... October 1966	*7th printing .. February 1970*
4th printing ... March 1968	*8th printing ...... June 1970*
5th printing .... August 1969	*9th printing ...... June 1970*

New Bantam edition / May 1971

2nd printing ... August 1971	*9th printing . November 1975*
3rd printing ... March 1972	*10th printing ..... June 1977*
4th printing . September 1972	*11th printing . December 1977*
5th printing .... August 1973	*12th printing ..... May 1978*
6th printing .. February 1974	*13th printing .. February 1979*
7th printing . September 1974	*14th printing .. January 1980*
8th printing .... August 1975	*15th printing ..... June 1980*
	16th printing ... November 1981

*Photograph of Louis L'Amour
by John Hamilton—Globe Photos, Inc.*

ISBN 0-553-20761-4

Published simultaneously in the United States and Canada

Bantam Books are published by Bantam Books, Inc. Its trademark, consisting of the words "Bantam Books" and the por-
trayal of a rooster, is Registered in U.S. Patent and Trademark
Office and in other countries. Marca Registrada. Bantam
Books, Inc., 666 Fifth Avenue, New York, New York 10103.

PRINTED IN THE UNITED STATES OF AMERICA

25 24 23 22 21 20

TO DUTCH SAM
WHO MISSED WHEN IT MATTERED

one

The man called Key-Lock was a man alone, and before him lay wilderness. Behind him were searching men, and each was armed, each carried a rope. Each rope was noosed for hanging, and each man was intent on the purpose of the chase.

The solitary rider did not fear his aloneness, for he had the companionship of the mind. He had strength also, patience beyond that of most men, and some knowledge of the wild lands into which he rode. If the men who pursued knew nothing of him, he at least knew their kind, and was stronger because of this.

They were men shaped and tempered to the harsh ways of a harsh land, strong in their sense of justice, ruthless in their demand for punishment, relentless in pursuit. In the desert and the wilderness they had built their homes, and from the desert and the wilderness they drew their courage and their code. And the desert knows no mercy, the wilderness shows no kindness.

Before the man called Key-Lock lay a land fragmented and torn, a magnificent land, gnarled and ancient. It was a land of shattered battlements, broken towers, and the headless figures of vast and shapeless gods. An empty land, yet crowded with epics in stone, harried by wind and thunderstorm, ripped by flash floods, blistered by summer's heat, frozen by winter's cold.

He rode now in Arizona, but beyond the horizon to the north lay Utah, and between himself and the border, a desert. Between himself and escape—if he chose to escape—lay an almost waterless waste in which he must trust to his ingenuity to keep him free.

The border lay ahead, but the border was merely a line on a map, and did not exist in the minds of the men who pursued him. If they knew of this border, it would have no place in their thinking, for to them he had already crossed another border, a border between the law and the lawless, between the right and the wrong, between what was done and what was not done.

To kill a man who faced you with a gun was in their minds no crime, nor was it a crime in the customs of their period. In the East and in Europe men settled affairs of honor with pistols, but according to plan and ritual. In the West, in what was a new world, where men were often strangers to each other, the settling of such an affair was immediate, and without ritual.

To shoot a man in the back, however, *was* a crime, and this they believed he had done, and for this he must be hung.

But it was not enough for the man called Key-Lock to understand the philosophy of the hunters; the important thing for him was to escape them.

Though he knew none of the men back there personally, he knew there must be good men among them, and on a different occasion he might have been riding as one of them, the pursuer instead of the pursued. For he had worked beside such men, fought beside them, and he knew that they were hard-working men, stern but just, according to their code. When such men come to a new land the law comes with them, for they are builders of homes, builders of towns, layers of foundations.

And now he must escape or fight. If he fought, he must be prepared to kill, and he had no enmity for these men ... not yet.

"Where's he bound?"

"Home, more'n likely. He'll need an outfit if he aims to run far ... if we don't get to him first."

"Where's he live?"

"He was a stranger, and had no trail outfit with him. Over to the store they said that when he taken out to get away, the one thing he latched onto was a woman's comb."

"A *comb?*"

"Seems daft, but that's what was told us. One of those fancy combs like Spanish women wear in their hair. He rummaged through all that grub and truck in the store just for that."

Kimmel's eyes narrowed against the sun's hard glare. "He's got him a good horse. Moves right along."

"Big buckskin," Chesney said. "I seen the horse. Wears a Key-Lock brand. A key alongside a keyhole—never seen it before."

For a few minutes silence rode among them, except for the beat of their horses' hoofs and the creak of saddle leather.

"He's covering ground, all right." Neill was the youngest of them, and he felt the need of words. He was also the latest to arrive in this part of the country—only four years ago.

Hardin was the best of them at reading sign, and from the first he had been disturbed that the rider had not put his horse to the run. He held him to a steady, distance-eating gait, but showed no inclination to make a sudden dash to get away. Studying those tracks, and reading what they indicated, Hardin had an uneasy feeling that they had brought themselves a packet of trouble.

"He's no tenderfoot." Chesney expressed the thought Hardin held. "He's covering ground, but he knows how to save a horse, and he knows wild country."

Dust lifted from the hoofs of their horses. The sun was hot upon their shoulders. The land was parched and baked. Dancing heat-waves promised water that was not there, and the distant blue of mountains a coolness they would not provide.

The trail lay straight before them. Only at clumps of rock or thorny brush did it swerve. Like a thrown lance, it seemed to thrust at the distant heart of the hills. The six men of the posse rode warily, their thoughts uneasy about what lay in the mind of the man they pursued.

You can know a man if you follow his trail, if you follow long enough. By his tracks on the land the ways of a man are made plain—his kindness or his cruelty, his ignorance or his cunning, his strength or his weakness. Many a man who could read not a word of print could read character, story, and plot from a pattern of tracks, and from the building of fires.

In the hours of riding since leaving the town of Freedom, these men had learned much, but they had much still to learn.

"What started it?" one of them asked now.

In the vast hollow of silence the words hung empty and alone.

Hardin turned his head in the manner of a man who rides much in the wind, and let the words drift back. As he spoke he shifted the rifle from one hand to the other to dry his sweaty palms upon his shirt front.

"Loose talk. He was buyin' grub in the Bon Ton an'

took offense at something Johnny said. Johnny was wearin' a gun, an' the Key-Lock man wasn't, so Johnny told him to go fill his hand or he'd hunt him down anyway.

"Johnny was in the saloon when he came back an' pushed the door open an' shot Johnny twice in the back whilst he stood drinkin' at the bar. Third shot busted a bottle of whiskey."

After a moment's silence, Neill asked slyly, "We hanging him for killing Johnny, or for busting the whiskey?"

It was a fair question, but the dignity of the riders and their mission was not to be lightened by humor. They offered no reply, nor any acknowledgment that he had spoken.

Neill's eyes wandered over the white and copper land, cut here and there by deep arroyos or ridged by the raw backs of ancient lava flows. He held no liking for the lynching of any man, and he knew nothing of the one for whom they hunted, beyond what had been told him. The men he rode with were his friends and neighbors, the men with whom he shared work and their few pleasures.

Like himself, they had come to this wild land bringing the potential of home, and homes demanded order and consideration for the rights of others, a recognition of the necessities of regulations and law. Their women folk came with them or followed after, bringing their own desires, among them the need for church and school, for human association.

The town of Freedom had only such law as its citizens chose to provide. If lawlessness was wary of Freedom, it was due to the fact that, as in most western towns, the butcher, the baker, and the banker were veterans of the War Between the States and the Indian wars. Every citizen had grown to manhood handling guns, and all were prepared to use such weapons when need be. The idea of some gunman or band of outlaws "treeing" a western town was known, but here it had never happened.

The James-Younger band tried it at Northfield and they were run out of town, shot to doll rags and leaving their dead behind; the Daltons tried it at Coffeyville, and the one man who survived had sixteen buckshot in him. There were a few other attempts, no more successful—often to the regret of the townspeople, for such attempts came under the head of entertainment in towns where there was not much of any other kind.

The gunman stayed to his side of town, like the gambler and the lady of light company, and was tolerated as long as he offered no trouble to the established citizenry.

Freedom was scarcely old enough to have the need to draw such a line, and as yet there was no law except such as was administered by themselves. However, they had all known Johnny, and Johnny had been shot in the back.

"Who saw the shooting?" Neill asked.

"Nobody saw it, actually. Sam was tendin' bar, but he was down at the other end and it happened too fast. But this Key-Lock man couldn't have given Johnny a chance. Johnny was too good with a gun."

Johnny, Neill recalled, was far better than just good with a gun. He was *damned* good, and prided himself on the fact. Neill felt a twinge of uneasiness, and then a faint sense of guilt that he should for an instant doubt anything that was said of Johnny; but he couldn't help recalling that Johnny was a little less than friendly to strangers.

The dust grew thicker, and Neill pulled his bandana up over his mouth and nose as the others had. His eyes sought the shimmering blue of those distant lakes. Enticing and lovely, they lay across the trail ahead and in the bottoms off to the right. They were mirage, but many a man had been led to his death by their ever-retreating shore lines.

Maybe there was water in those heat waves if a man only knew how to extract it. The thought drew his hand to his canteen, where the slosh of water was inviting, but he knew that by this time the water was warm and brackish, and too little of it remained. Moreover, none of the older men had yet shown any inclination to drink.

"Will you know him if you see him, Kimmel?" Chesney asked.

"He's a big man, maybe on the lean side, but strong-made. Maybe thirty-five. No hand to talk about his business, but over to the store where he did his buying folks said he shaped up like a mighty hard piece of merchandise."

Chesney himself was a wiry man with strong brown hands. He was hard as a whipstock, with bits of sharp steel for eyes. He had built his outfit carefully, driving in a few head when he first came, and tending them like a dairy herd through the first season. He was a good man and a good neighbor, but there was no give in him. He was stubborn in his opinions and a driver, pushing hard on himself and all about him. He had been the first to reach Neill's place that time when a prairie fire threatened.

Kimmel had been a close second, racing his wagon as if it was a buckboard, and it was filled with sacking already wet, and with shovels. Last year when Hardin was laid up with a broken leg, Kimmel fed Hardin's stock and his own too, all through a hard winter, and he had a long ride every day to do it.

Chesney and Johnny had been saddle partners on the old Squaw Mountain round-ups, and when Chesney drove his small herd into this part of the country, Johnny had come along to see him through, then located a place of his own and stayed on.

Johnny Webb had been a dare-devil and a hellion, but he was well liked for all of that. He laughed a lot, played practical jokes, and was ready to break a horse for anybody just for the hell of it. He was fast with a gun, and no man was likely to beat him in a fair, stand-up shooting.

When Neill had come into the country, he had quickly realized the kind of community he had entered and he built solid friendships. There was a lot he did not know about the West, for back in Ohio he had been a farmer, but he was catching on fast. When they invited him to be a posse member he knew he had been accepted and was one of them. It was an honor to ride beside such men into what might become a shooting affair.

Neill stared at the tracks of the big buckskin and felt a queer sensation when he realized the rider of that horse might soon be dead, hung by the neck, and Neill's own hand would be on that rope.

He had never killed a man—not even an Indian—nor seen one killed. He was probably the only man in the group of whom that could be said.

Now Johnny Webb was gone, Johnny with his laughter and his jokes, brightening more than one day's work on the range. And Neill was feeling guilty at remembering that he had never really liked Johnny, and that there had been strain between them when Neill first came into this part of the country. It was only after Chesney accepted him, and after Johnny apparently realized that Neill was not a potential rival that a sort of friendship developed.

Johnny might have been a little overanxious with that gun, Neill thought, but he deserved something better than a shot in the back.

"He's afoot," Chesney said suddenly, "leadin' his horse."

"He's a big man," Hardin said, "and he figures to give us a long chase."

"His horse has gone lame, maybe," McAlpin suggested.

"No, that horse doesn't limp. He's just a canny one, that's all."

A mile fell behind them, and then another mile.

The deep dust gave way to a parched dry plain of desert sand. Hardin indicated a couple of flecks on the sand-crust where something had spilled. "Water," he said.

"He'll need that water," Neill said. "He'd best go easy with it."

"Bet you a dollar he was wipin' out his horse's nostrils," Chesney said. "Dust interferes with a horse's breathing, and a man could kill a horse, runnin' him on this flat."

The man they pursued was not running his horse, but if they caught up with him, he would have to run. Neill mopped his brow, and wiped the sweat-band of his hat. He thought of his wife and the milk she kept in a stone jug in the well. It would taste almighty good about now.

Suddenly he looked at the sun. It had been on the left, but now it was on the right, for the trail had swerved sharply. Hardin, who was riding point, swore.

Riding up beside him, the men found themselves looking into a draw that cracked the desert's face only a few rods away. There was a place where a horse had been tethered, and a bit of white fluttered from a rock.

Chesney rode down into the draw to pick it up, and they heard him swear again. Scrambling his horse back up the draw, he passed the paper to Hardin. It looked like a leaf torn from a tally book. On it a message was scrawled.

That was a fair shootin anyway six ain't nowhars enuf. go fetch more men. man on the gray better titen his cinch or heel have him a sore backed hoss.

The note was unsigned.

"Why, the low-livin' skunk!" Short spoke half under his breath. "Not forty yards off, and him with a rifle."

Neill, his face flushed with anger, was tightening his cinch. Nobody appeared to notice him; they were as embarrassed as he was himself. The note was an insult to all of them, even if the advice was good.

They were angry men, but they were frightened men, too. It gave them an eerie feeling to realize that the man they were hunting had been lying within easy range, close enough to kill one or more of them before they could either attack or take shelter.

The man was playing Injun with them, and they did not like it. Their dignity was offended, but more than that, they realized they had been grossly negligent. They had taken it for granted the man was out there in front of them, running.

"Fair shootin', hell!" McAlpin said. "Right in the back!"

They went ahead now with increased caution. Their quarry had circled about and allowed them to pass, and he might be watching close by even now. Until this moment they had been the hunters; now they felt that they themselves were hunted.

Deliberately, the man they sought was using every trick to make pursuit more difficult. The note had the effect of slowing them to the slowest of walks. They must pause, circle each place of possible ambush, proceed with utmost watchfulness. Each time they took these precautions they found nothing, yet each time they might have been met with a bullet.

Now the trail took them into the bottom of a wash where the fitful puffs of wind they had met occasionally on the flat desert were gone. The wash was an oven, its floors and walls reflecting savage heat. They seemed to be riding through flames that seared and burned. Eyes smarting from the salt of their sweat, skin itching from the dust that caked the stubble on their jaws, they clung to the trail. As they went along, Hardin studied each wall with care, searching for some point at which their man might have escaped.

Suddenly the wash turned into an apron of sand that went down into the vast basin of a dry lake, white with alkali. Yet the lake was not entirely dry, for in the center was a sheet of water, the result of recent rains. The dead water was heavy with alkali.

The man called Key-Lock had ridden his horse into the water. The tracks were there, and they stared at them, blinking the sweat from their eyes.

"He daren't ride across that," Hardin commented. "Out there in the middle it would be too deep, and he could bog down."

Their party split, three circling the lake in either direction, seeking tracks. They had gone only a few hundred yards when Neill glanced back to see Chesney's uplifted arm, calling them back. He had found where the horse and rider had left the water.

The ruse was a simple one, but it was a delaying tactic that gave advantage to the pursued. Neill felt his anger rising. The man was playing them, playing them like fish on a line.

In the beginning Neill had hoped to have it over and be back at the ranch tonight, but as the hours went by it had become obvious that their chase was not to prove so easy. The time consumed, even their choice of a camp, would not be left to them. It would be dictated by the man they hunted. He knew where he would go, and when, while they did not know and could not know. It was clear now that his intent was to discourage them. Deliberately, he was choosing the roughest country, the worst trails.

The line of hoof prints veered sharply to the left, pointing through thick brush toward the shoulder of the mountain.

"Where the devil's he goin'?" Chesney demanded irritably. "This doesn't make sense."

No one answered him. Strung out in single file, they rode on, sagging with weariness. Suddenly Kimmel, who was in the lead now, pulled up short. Before them a thread of water trickled from the rocks into a basin of stones.

"I'll be damned for a coyote!" Hardin exclaimed. "I never knew this was here."

Kimmel swung down, and the others followed. "I can use a drink," he said. Indicating the small stone basin, he added, "Somebody put in a sight of work here. This hasn't been built long."

Hardin had been scouting around, studying the tracks, old and new. All were made by the same horse and the same man. "Fixed it himself. Wonder how he located it in the first place?"

"Looks to me like he knows this country," Short said.

Hardin chuckled, eyes glinting with a hard humor. "We hooked onto a real old he-coon, boys. This one's from the high timber. Now, we know it takes no time for a man and a horse to drink, but it takes a while for six horses and six men to drink. That little basin will need time to refill before we can all water up."

"He ain't missed a trick," Kimmel said.

"D'you think he'll stand and make a fight of it?" McAlpin asked.

"He'll fight," Chesney said. "This one will fight, and I hope he does."

Hardin shot him a glance. "You read that sign like I do?" he asked quietly. "If you do, you know what's comin'."

Neill put his tongue to dry lips. He looked from one to the other. A change had come over them now, and fear touched him with cold fingers.

This man was sure of himself. He had told them it was a fair shooting, but that note had been a warning if anything ever was. The fact that he could have had them within easy range told them what he might have done. He could have shot them like fish in a barrel, but when he chose to fight he would choose his ground, and theirs.

Neill was no coward, but when he thought about his wife alone on the ranch, he felt sick. He might die today, and she could never make it alone. She would have to give up the ranch, and all their plans together. She would have to go back to her folks, and would have to sell everything to raise money for the trip. How long since he had seen any cash money?

By now the glare had faded and softened. The desert sunset bathed the land in a pastel radiance mingled with fingers of shadow. Out on the desert, a quail called. Another, somewhere to their right, replied.

We could quit, Neill thought. *We could quit now before it's too late.*

But he did not speak this thought aloud, nor would any of the others, even if they thought it. Something had been started, and they must carry it through. The law must not be flouted, the sinful must pay for their sins.

"It's like he had a goddam string on us," Chesney complained.

From the beginning the hunted man had been in command, from the beginning he had led them on. Most escaping men think only of escape; they do not make plans for the pursuers. This man should have been running scared, he should have been hunting a hole somewhere, but he was doing no such thing. He was desert-wise, and he was in no hurry. He was borrowing time when he felt it necessary, but he was choosing his own course and his own gait.

Into the minds of each man crept an uneasy thought: Sooner or later he would have them where he wanted them, *and then what?* How many would die?

But now their pride was involved, their pride as well as their code, and their code said that for a life taken as Johnny's had been, a life must be paid.

Neill's thoughts turned again to his wife. She would be feeding the baby now, wondering where he was, and keeping the food warm. None of them had expected this to be anything but a short chase, with perhaps a brief gun battle at the end.

Regretfully, Neill realized that now it might be a week before he got home—if he ever did.

two

The trail they followed led across starkly eroded foothills dotted with clumps of cedar and Spanish bayonet. It was a weird and broken land where long fingers of black lava stretched out toward the dry lake they had left behind. Ahead of them rose a low mesa.

The Key-Lock man was in no hurry, and he traveled like an Indian, taking the longest route if it was the easiest on his horse. Each of the pursuers was worried by this in his secret mind. What could lie before this man that gave him such confidence?

Chesney topped out on the mesa and drew up to give his horse a breather, and they all gathered about him, studying the country. Hard-working men, they had been held to their own range by the demands of water and cattle, and the need to get something started; none of them had ever ridden so far to the north as this.

"Hardin, what do you think he's got in his mind?"

Chesney asked. "So far's I know, there's nothin' off where he's bound. Just nothin' at all."

"He can't go west ... the canyon's thataway, and without wings he couldn't go any further." Hardin rinsed his mouth with a meager gulp of water, then swallowed it. "We don't think there's anything up there, but maybe he knows different." He hung the canteen carefully on the saddle horn. "We've sure bought ourselves an old he-coon, and he ain't goin' to be took easy."

"Took, hell!" Chesney exploded. "I'll see the man hang! I'll see him hang before ever I ride into Freedom again!"

Chesney meant just what he said, and it showed in each line of his hard-boned face. A good friend, he was a bitter, unrelenting enemy. And the man called Key-Lock had killed his best friend.

Neill was puzzled by his own feelings. He knew the need for law and order, and where no official law existed the citizens themselves were responsible, unless they wished to live in complete anarchy. He accepted the logic of the idea, but held no enthusiasm for the immediate situation. Like many another man, he preferred going about his own affairs, sitting at supper with his wife, smelling the good cooking smells, feeling the slow comfort of evening, the welcome release of the bed that awaited.

He looked almost enviously at Chesney, Hardin, and the others. Why didn't he feel as dedicated as they did?

Certainly, no man's life or property could be safe unless there was a rigidly enforced law, and he realized almost with shame that he wished this job was being done without him. He knew the law was every man's concern, but it was high time they elected a marshal.

This mesa on which they stood was at least a quarter of a mile square. Here and there a horse's hoof had left a white scar upon the surface, but it took them more than half an hour to find where their man had left the rock.

Hardin chuckled in appreciation as they followed the trail down. "Took him only a few minutes, so he gained good time on us. Long as he can do that, he don't have to run."

Shadows gathered in the low places as the sky took on a pattern of amazing colors. This was a corner of what was called the Painted Desert. Crossing a wide wash, they came out onto a desert of almost endless dunes. Beyond, rock pinnacles rose, and a mesa that loomed a good thousand feet above the desert.

"Lucky he ain't layin' for us. We'd get picked off like flies," Hardin said.

At that moment there came a smashing report followed by an angry whine, and the men broke and fled for shelter.

Short simply rolled from his saddle, and crawled behind a hummock of sand. His horse stood where his master had left him, and the canteen made a large hump behind the saddle. Suddenly the horse leaped to the solid *thud* of a bullet.

Short swore viciously. "If he's killed that horse, I'll—"

But the horse, shifting nervously, stood ground-hitched where the reins had fallen. A trickle of water ran from the punctured canteen.

There was nothing at which to fire. Their eyes searched the dunes, but there was no movement, no sign of life. The setting sun glared full into their eyes. Their trail had swung around a dune, the shot coming from their rear. Had he circled around them? Or had he been lying in wait when they rode past?

The trickle of water slowed to a slow drip. A bullet that could puncture a canteen could do as much for a man's skull.

Every man among them thought of what that emptied canteen might mean. They had filled their canteens at the spring, and it should be water enough, but only the man they pursued knew where they would be going, and he would not have emptied that canteen without reason.

They lay where they had dropped, and they waited. It was hot, but the creeping shadows brought a measure of coolness to the men in the shelter of the dunes.

"He's long gone," McAlpin said at last. Nobody showed any inclination to test the matter, so he thrust his own hat just past a rock. Nothing happened. But when he gave up and withdrew the hat, a bullet struck the sand nearby, a message from the Key-Lock man that he was still there, but that he was not to be fooled by such an obvious trick.

Their horses dozed in the sun. The warm sand under their bodies made it seem warmer still. Neill was bone-tired and he was glad of the rest. He had worked his body into a thin edging of shadow and was trying to relax.

When half an hour had gone by, Hardin began a flanking movement, crawling around the dunes. He vanished from sight, and after what seemed a long time, Neill was started from a doze by a long halloo. He could see Hardin standing where the shots had been fired, waving them on. One by one they went to their horses and mounted, then rode to the dune where Hardin waited for them.

On a bare shelf of sand stood three brass cartridge shells, neatly lined up. Nearby was a crude arrow formed from stones, and beside it, scratched in the hard-packed sand, were the words: *Foller the signs.*

Chesney jerked off his hat and threw it to the ground. "Why, that dirty, no-good—!" The words trailed off as he scuffed his foot through the message written in the sand.

"He's makin' light of us," Short said bitterly. "That damn' back-shootin' killer's goin' to pay for this!"

They started on again, their quarry's horse leaving

a plain trail, here and there deliberately marked by an arrow of broken branches or stones.

They were serious men riding on serious business, and the seeming levity, if not contempt, added to their irritation. Now the matter was becoming personal with each of them, for not only was the man evading them with success, but he was taunting their inability to catch up. The worst of it was, such a horse as the killer rode, handled with such care, might go on for days, even for weeks.

The vast basin was now behind them, lost in the misty purple of distance. The sun was going down, but all could see ahead of them the message chalked on the rock wall in big, sweeping letters. The flat piece of chalk rock with which it had been written lay in plain sight below:

Shade, so you won't get sun stroke.

Tired and surly, they merely stared at it without comment. The shadows lengthened, and their horses moved on without eagerness. In the desert air was a growing chill. Neill, riding at the end of the line, turned in his saddle to look back.

Behind them lay an enormous sweep of country, the mountain ridges and the edge of the escarpment touched by gold, the sky shot with great arrows of crimson. The desert's purple had grown deeper, and black shadows crouched in the open jaws of the canyons. Far away back there his wife would be at the door, looking up the trail toward town. Soon, despairing of his return, she would feed the stock they kept in the corral and then would go inside and feed the baby. She would eat alone, still watching the trail.

Before them, he thought, the days might stretch on and on, and suddenly he was shaken by a strange premonition that none of them would ever see Freedom again.

Who was this strange man who rode ahead of them, taunting them, but never deliberately trying to kill? Was it logical that a man who had shot another in the back would act in this way?

Kimmel and McAlpin, who had been riding side by side, halted suddenly, and the others rode up and gathered around. Before them on the trail an arrow of stones pointed down to a narrow, forbidding cleft in the rock; a chill wind blew from it, adding to their misgivings. Once within that cleft, where the walls lifted several hundred feet on either side, there would be no turning back, nor could more than one man at a time ride into the narrow space.

Kimmel dug into his shirt pocket for the makings and rolled a careful cigarette, his narrowed eyes studying the cleft, the cliffs above it, the rocks around.

"What do you think, Hardin?"

"Well, he ain't tried it yet, but if he's goin' to make a stand, this could be the place. A good man with a rifle could do about as he had a mind to, once he got us in there."

"I don't think he wants to."

Neill spoke without thinking, and the words hung in the still air.

"What's that mean?" Chesney sounded belligerent.

"I don't know." Whatever Neill's reasons, they weakened under Chesney's hard stare. "Only he's had chances. Seems to me if he wanted to kill somebody he could have done it. I'd say he's wasting a lot of time."

The others ignored him, and he withdrew into himself. Nevertheless, having said it, he wanted to bolster his argument with facts. Only he did not speak them aloud. *Why*, he told himself, *he had us dead to rights when he left that first note. He could have killed at least some of us, and when we hunted cover he could have taken out.*

That canteen shot ... he had been a good three hundred yards off when he fired, and it was a clean hit. No sooner had Neill considered this idea than he asked himself how, at that distance, he could have known it was a canteen? Did he have field glasses? And as soon as this occurred to him he was convinced of it. Not many men had field glasses, but here and there some ex-soldier had them, or might have picked them up by swapping around an army post.

It gave him a queer feeling to think that the man might even now be looking right into their faces, or reading their lips as they talked.

"The hell with it!" Hardin exclaimed suddenly, and shucking his Winchester he rode down into the gloomy cleft. There was nothing to do but to follow.

Immediately it was dark. The rock walls crowded in on either side. Neill's stirrup brushed the wall from time to time, and he could see nothing either before or behind him. Only when he looked up could he see the narrow strip of sky, far above, and occasionally a star.

Momentarily he feared the racketing boom of a shot in the narrow passage, but it did not come. After riding for some time and after several winding turns, they saw gray light before them, and then a bright star. Only it was not a star—it was a campfire.

As they emerged from the passage they spread out quickly and advanced in a mounted skirmish line, rifles ready.

There were scattered trees about, and some low brush, rendering their view indistinct. Chesney was the first to reach the campfire, and the sound of his swearing shattered the stillness like the splintering of glass.

Beside a running stream a small fire had been built, and near it was a supply of additional fuel. On a bit of paper, weighted with two stones, was a small mound of coffee, and a smaller mound of sugar.

They stared at the scene, choked by bitterness. The taunt was obvious. They were being nursed along like a pack of tenderfeet.

"I'll be double-damned if I will!" Short exclaimed angrily.

Hardin was more philosophical. "Might as well make the most of it. We can't trail him at night anyway."

Kimmel brought a coffeepot from his gear and dipped water from the stream. Kimmel was a practical man, and he liked his coffee.

They stripped the rigs from their horses and picketed them on the grass of a meadow close by. There was little enough in their saddlebags, for none of them had expected a long chase, and they must ride on short rations to make them last. Neill looked at the small pile of sugar enviously, wishing he might hide some of it to carry home to his wife. It had been a long time since she had tasted real sugar.

Short, his burst of anger gone, was staring about in an odd manner. He looked from the flowing water to the pool into which it fell. "Boys, I know this place," he said. "I've heard tell of it many's the time. This here is Mormon Well."

Hardin had been feeding twigs into the fire. Now he stood back and looked carefully around, measuring what he saw against what he had heard in the towns and the cow camps. Towering cliffs on three sides of a bowl, the clustered trees, the meadow. "Yes, I think you're right," he agreed. "It could be."

"Now, why d' you suppose he led us *here?*" McAlpin asked.

Neill glanced from face to face. "What's Mormon Well, I never heard of it."

Nobody replied, but Short walked around the pool. "Why, the damned fool!" he said. "He's led us right to it! I'd lay a dollar to a doughnut he's never even heard the story."

Hardin's eyes were grimly amused. He repeated McAlpin's question. "Why do you suppose he led us here?"

Chesney was sour. "That Mormon Well story is just whiskey talk."

"Like hell it is!" Short's temper flared. "I've seen gold from that cache—seen it with my own eyes! Held it right in my hand!" He thrust out an open hand, then closed it to a hard fist. "Within a few miles of this place there's more gold than a man's likely to see in a lifetime!"

"*Gold?*" Neill's voice was startled.

"You know the story better'n any of us, Bill," McAlpin suggested. "You tell him."

"I ain't about to. Damn it, can't you see what he's tryin' to do? If we start huntin' that gold we'll split up and forget all about him, then he's gone scot-free."

"A dozen men have died huntin' for this well, and here we are, Johnny-on-the-spot."

Johnny . . .

They fell silent, but after a while Short said, "Well, we can always come back to it. We can hang him and then come back." There was an obvious lack of enthusiasm in his tone.

McAlpin stirred. "You ever heard of anybody who left this place and ever found it again? Not even the ones who hid the gold. This here Mormon Well has always been the joker in the deck."

"Use your heads!" Chesney was irritable. "Who would lead us right to the gold when he could have it all for himself?"

"I don't know what you're talking about," Neill said. "Is there gold buried somewhere about?"

Hardin chuckled ironically. "He's going to get clean away. He surely is."

"What *are* you?" Chesney demanded angrily. "A passel of youngsters who'll go chasin' after any red wagon comes along? We started out to hang a man!"

"I wish somebody would tell me the story," Neill protested.

"Bill," Hardin suddenly said to Chesney, "do you remember Gay Cooley?"

"What about him?"

"Gay knew this country, and he spent years huntin' the Lost Wagons. He knew this country better than the Navajos did. Now, if this here is Mormon Well, then right over there is Marsh Pass." Hardin drew a rough pattern on the sand with a twig. "If this Key-Lock man is going east or northeast he will head for that pass. Otherwise he has to cross the river, and there's only two places he can do that, both of them west of here.

"Lee's Ferry," he went on, and indicated it on the map, "is away over northwest, and the Crossing of the Fathers is northwest, too, only not so far. My hunch is he's about to double back and make for the Crossing of the Fathers."

Neill started to interrupt, then held his peace, watching Chesney, who was studying the sand map. Either way, their man was reaching for the wildest kind of country, but he was hemmed in by the canyons of the Colorado and the San Juan.

"We might head him off," Short suggested.

"In this country?" Hardin said. "We lose his trail and we've lost him entirely."

"Maybe not," Neill suggested. "I'm thinking of that comb."

"Comb?"

"Sure ... the one thing he took out of all those supplies he had to leave behind so's he could run. The one thing he chose to take was that fancy comb. Seems to me that means he's got him a woman somewhere, and that he figures to see her, chased as he is, or not."

Hardin looked at Neill. "Now, that's a good thought. You're right, Neill."

Neill was embarrassed, but he was pleased. Chesney was staring at the map, but now a new thought was in his mind. Hardin hunched over the map, too. "If he has a woman cached up here somewhere, he'll surely go to her. Now, where would a man be likely to have a woman? One who would treasure a fancy comb?"

"That's any woman, Hardin." Neill had gained courage. "Womenfolks have a liking for fancy things. Some woman set her heart on that comb, you can bet, or else he set his heart on giving it to her."

"I don't agree," Kimmel said. "No man in his right mind would leave a woman alone in this country. Not if he had to leave her for maybe a week or more."

"What else could he do?"

They were thinking now. They knew the problems of a man with a woman on a lonely ranch. They understood his problem, but with them it was different—they had each other. If one of them had to leave the ranch there was always a neighbor to stop by and see that all went well. They were together even when alone, for they shared their dangers, their emergencies. But what of this man? Who was there in the country ahead who might stand by in case of need?

Reluctantly each one of them began to harbor the thought that if this man was alone he was no ordinary man; and if he left his woman alone, she was no ordinary woman, either.

"When we find him," Hardin suggested, "he may not be alone. Maybe he's leading us right into an ambush. Maybe that's why he ain't worried."

Short looked up at Hardin, his face revealing his shock. The same thought was suddenly in the minds of all. They had started out to hang a man—suppose all of them were killed in the process? Neill felt a queer coldness in his belly at the thought of his wife back there alone on the ranch. What had he gotten himself into, anyway?

After a while Chesney spoke. "Boys, we've got to look at it this way. We've got to have law in this country. We've got to serve notice that we take care of our own. If we don't, there ain't no one of us going to last out the year."

Neill's mind had slipped away from the chase,

seeking refuge in a dream of what might be, when he knew he could not escape what was. He was thinking of those wagonloads of gold. Why, with his share he could build a fine house, buy fine furniture. They could have sugar in the house, and tea. Emma felt the need for tea—tea was elegant, to her way of thinking. Out here a body had mighty little that was nice, let alone elegant; and Emma was forever talking of how her Boston ancestors had done things.

"I wonder who he is—the Key-Lock man?" Neill said.

"It don't make a passel of difference," Chesney said. "Far's I'm concerned, he's just a man we're fixin' to hang."

three

She came up from the water and stopped at the edge of the pool to wring out her long blonde hair. She moved with a natural grace and with no shrinking at her nakedness. Her body was white, and unbelievably lovely in the cool morning air.

Never had she known such stillness. Even the waterfall seemed only to rustle faintly as it dropped into the pool and lost itself in widening ripples.

It was music she missed most of all, but music of the kind she wanted to hear was gone from her life. She had left all that behind in that other world that seemed so far away, almost as if it were on a distant star. Music was gone, unless she learned to listen as he did.

"Listen, Kristina," he had said, "you have only to listen. There is music on the wind."

One heard it best on the high plateaus, on Skeleton Mesa or over by Tall Mountain. The canyons had music of another kind. And wherever the winds blew, they smelled faintly of cedar or sage, but sometimes only of heat.

All this land, she felt, was haunted by memories; not memories of her own, for she had come only lately to this region of stark and lonely cliffs, nor were they memories of his, for he had been here only once before. The memories were those of the long-vanished people who had lived in this place, whose dwellings lined each almost inaccessible crack in the canyon wall. She thought of them often, and felt somehow akin to them. What would he say when she told him that?

She had been a silly fool, a wild, silly fool to go riding off with a man she knew not at all, into an utter wilderness. With a man who had come in out of the night and the storm, and had merely looked at her across the room and claimed her for his own.

"Who are you?" she had asked that night.

His eyes never wavered from hers. "That is a foolish question," was his answer. "You have known for two minutes who I am, and what you are going to do."

"And what am I going to do?"

"Ride away with me before the sun rises," he said, "and be married when we find a minister worthy of the name."

He had shouldered past her, so close she could smell the woodsmoke that clung to his buckskins, the woodsmoke of cedar, mingled with the smell of pine and horse.

He had crossed to the fire and held out his strong brown hands to the flames, and she had seen Neerland look at him with a cold, still attention, and she had been afraid.

Afraid not for herself but for this stranger, who could not know Neerland, as she herself had not known him when she came west to meet him.

She had crossed the room then, and sat down behind Neerland's shoulder, telling herself that this was the man she had come to marry. Yet although her eyes were cast down toward the flames, her mind followed the movements of the stranger.

Behind her someone asked, low-voiced, "Who's that?"

"Never saw him before. Horse wears a Key-Lock brand." And then after a moment, "Never heard of that, either."

Her eyes lifted her heart from the lonely place where it had held itself during these past days. Her heart in her eyes, she looked at the Key-Lock man, his hands reaching toward the flames.

He was tall, with powerful shoulders. She was a girl from a land of strong men, and she knew the bodies and the movements of men from seeing many at work or climbing beside her in the mountains. She looked at him, appraising the strength of him. He was not so big as Neerland, but he would be strong, she knew, very strong. She noted the way the muscles of his shoulders bulged the buckskin jacket. He wore a gun, but so did they all, and a bowie knife. Both knife scabbard and the gun holster were tied down.

There were nine men in that room, and three women besides herself, and she knew the men stared at her, but she was accustomed to that. She was pure blonde, and taller than many men. Her body was lithe and strong, for since childhood she had climbed mountains, skied down the long mountain slopes in her own northern land, and ridden horses in every country of Europe, even with the fine horsemen of Hungary.

She knew what she was and who she was, but she did not know where she was going, nor what was to become of her. And the life from which she had come was a far cry from this one into which she was going.

These people had their pride, a pride of being and of doing, a pride of having chosen to go west, to challenge the country, the Indians, and the wilderness. Her pride was an ancient one, so much a part of her being that she was not even conscious of it. She was of the nobility ... how foolish that sounded here!

Her father had been a diplomat, a man known and respected both for his ancient lineage and his own abilities, a man of importance in all the capitals of the Continent. And now he was dead, and the fault lay with her, if fault there was.

Of course, it was a man. She had met him in Vienna, and again in Paris, and she had fallen in love with him. Or she thought she had, which amounted to the same thing. The trouble was, the man was married, but this she did not know. He had spoken of her in a slighting manner and her father heard. A challenge followed, and her father was killed.

It was then that she fled Europe, fled all she knew and loved. There was no more family, although there were estates. She had fled ... but not before she had gone to see her lover one last time.

She had gone to him, and she had entered by the door he often left open. He was standing there at the sideboard.

"Kristina!" He was amazed, and turned slightly toward her, holding a bottle and a glass. He started to speak again, but she interrupted.

The night was bitter cold, and she closed the door behind her. She held her head high and looked at him across the room.

"My father had no son to horsewhip you as you deserve," she said, "and my father was an old man, whose hand was not steady."

"Kristina!" he exclaimed again, staring at her.

"Mine will be steady," she said; and raising the pistol, she looked coolly down the barrel, and shot him. She threw the pistol on the floor and left.

A friendly fisherman, with whom she had often gone on the sea as a child, carried her across to the coast of Denmark. And from Denmark she had sailed to America.

And now she was here in this strange place. She was here at this stage stop where she had come to meet the man she had agreed to marry. She had first met Oskar Neerland in the East; he had spoken her language, guessed what she might have been; and, with her money gone, she had accepted his proposal. He must go west first, he said, then she would come to join him and they would be married.

The room they were in now was long and low, with a fireplace at one end. The room had a stuffy warmth. In here there was a crude bar, and in the two adjoining rooms were a few beds ... one room was for women, one for men. Out back were corrals and a lean-to stable.

She had turned her eyes away suddenly from the back of the Key-Lock man, and Neerland was watching her. She had seen that same look in his eyes that afternoon, shortly after her arrival. She had seen that expression when he battered his horse with a gauntleted fist, striking it cruelly while he gripped the bit tight in his hand.

He looked at her, then looked away, his eyes going to the stranger who now turned and walked to the bar. For an instant she had believed Neerland would speak to him.

"So you like his looks, do you?" Neerland said with a sneer. "He's nothing. Just a drifter, a saddle tramp."

She kept silent, and her silence angered him.

"When I get you out to my place I'll knock some of that fancy feeling out of you," he said, "and take pleasure in it."

"I may not go."

He laughed. "You'll go, all right. You came here to marry me, and there's nobody to stand between us. Not even if they wanted to ... nobody."

She looked at him directly with her wide blue eyes, and she said quietly, "I can look after myself. I need no help."

"*You?*" The word was contemptuous.

She merely continued looking at him, her smooth

face revealing nothing. Then she turned her back on him and went over to the fire.

He lunged from the bench where he sat and grasped her shoulder, spinning her hard around, his hand drawn back.

"Leave her alone."

Neerland's hand held, and slowly lowered. Then he turned, his eyes holding a hot eagerness. The Key-Lock man was turning toward him, but Neerland realized with a shock that it was not he who had spoken, but the manager of the station.

He was a slender man, no longer young, with a face in which only the eyes seemed to live. A shotgun lay across the top of the bar, and one hand rested on it.

"You talking to *me?*"

"To you. I said leave her alone. No man mistreats a lady on these premises."

Neerland shrugged contemptuously. "She won't be here long. I am taking her with me."

The station manager's eyes did not leave Neerland when he spoke to her. "Ma'am, if you don't want to go, you don't have to. Is he your man?"

"No."

"Ask her how she got here," Neerland said.

"I came to marry him. I did not know he was the way I saw him today, and a man who beats a horse would try to beat a woman."

Neerland turned his eyes on her. "*Try?*"

"You would try, I am sure, and then I would kill you."

There was silence in the room. Something in the way she spoke told everyone present that she meant exactly what she said.

Though she continued to look at Neerland, her words were for the man in the buckskin hunting jacket. "I am a stranger to your country, and I have never known hardship, but for a man who would love me and be gentle, I would face anything. You, Mr. Neerland, are not that man."

The stranger straightened from the bar and swept off his hat. "Ma'am," he said quietly, "if you'll ride with me in the morning, there's a sky pilot—a minister—about sixty miles west. I should be most honored."

Across the room their eyes met and held for a long moment of silence, and then she said, "I will ride with you, sir. I will ride beside you in the morning."

Neerland started to speak, then was silent, and turning abruptly away, he went outside.

The station manager returned his shotgun to its place under the bar. "You've got a good woman there, mister," he said. "Give her time to know the country."

Suddenly embarrassed, the Key-Lock man crossed the room to her, and the others turned away, granting them what little privacy the room allowed.

"I am going into new land," he said. "I have no ranch, no home. I am going to a place I know, a place where a man can build."

"All right."

"You have your things with you?"

"Yes." She gestured to the pile in the corner. Surreptitiously the eyes of the women followed her hand's movement. "It is too much, I am afraid."

The Key-Lock man looked at the expensive valise, the small trunk, the other things. "We will manage," he said.

"That was good advice," he said, as they rode westward. His eyes were on the trail before them. "To give you time to know the country."

He gave her time, and she needed it, for everything was strange. There was nothing here that in any way resembled the life she had known, that in any way reflected what she had been. These stark and lonely mountains were not like the mountains of her own beloved north country.

"Give them time, too," he said, "and they become a part of you."

He had bought three extra pack mules for her things alone, as many as for their whole outfit. But he had not complained, and he had packed her things with care.

"You may throw them out if you wish," she had said. "What they represent is behind me."

"They are yours," he replied gently. "It is good to have familiar things with you."

They were married in a quiet ceremony in a bare desert town. The minister was a quiet man, and a sincere one, and he was part of this land, too. And that night they slept side by side, but not together.

When they rode on again next morning, she noticed that again and again he turned to look behind him.

"You expect someone?" she asked.

"In this country? But you must always expect someone or something."

The long riding tired her but it did not sap her strength, and after the third day she was no longer even tired.

She had known enough of camping to appreciate his skill, and she came to realize that no move was wasted, that nothing was left to chance, that all of his constant awareness was so much a part of him that he no longer even thought of it.

On the fourth night he looked across the fire at her. "Some day there will be a visitor," he said.

She waited, for she had never been given to unnecessary words.

"Neerland," he said.

With sudden fear, she knew he was right. She had almost forgotten Neerland. He was not far behind them, only a few days away, but all her feelings, all her thoughts, all her own awareness had been given to this country and this man. And she was coming to know him.

"You have not asked where we will go," he said.

"I go with you."

He added a few sticks to the small fire. "It is a place where no one comes, only the Navajos sometimes."

"They are Indians?"

He nodded. "Long ago, perhaps several hundred years ago, there were other Indians there. In the cliffs they built houses that are still there. After a long time they went away, I do not know why."

"What will you do there?"

"Run some cattle, when I can afford them. Build a place of my own—a place for us."

He talked of this, and of the land toward which they rode. He talked easily, and well. She, who had known so many men of education, men adept with words, saw that he, too, knew their uses.

He seemed to understand what she was thinking, but he said nothing of himself; he only said, "Don't misunderstand the men you meet. Many are uneducated in your way, but they know much else. They have an education that fits them for living *here*. There will be others who may have traveled widely ... I hunted buffalo with a man who attended Gottingen University, and I soldiered with a graduate of the Sorbonne. Yet both of them talked 'western,' using all the easy phrases, the rough talk of the cow camps."

Later, when they had left the trail that went west and were weaving their way north into the wild land of desert and canyon, she asked, "Do you think he will find us?"

"Sooner or later," he answered.

How long ago had that been? Weeks now, but she had forgotten time. In this place it seemed a meaningless thing.

Now she stood beside the water and dried herself on a piece of torn blanket that she used for a towel, and then she dressed herself, taking her time. Close beside her was the Winchester he had given her.

"Can you shoot?" he had asked her.

"Yes," she had said. Then after a minute she had added, "Do not be afraid. I shall not shoot until I see what I am to hit, and when I shoot, I shall hit what I am shooting at."

Two days later he had ridden away.

He had paused at the last. "If anything happens to me that I cannot return, ride out of here and ride west. It is a long way, but stay on the trail until you see the sign for Prescott."

"All right," she said. And then she lifted her blue eyes to his. "How long shall I wait?"

"Two weeks, at least. I could almost crawl it in that time."

He had been gone for fifteen days. So time meant something after all.

four

Chesney drew up to study the country. Behind them lay the gigantic wall of cliffs through which they had ridden the evening before. To the north the ridge stretched away as far as the eye could follow, and on the east of it, where they now were, the rugged country was dotted with cedar. To the south, beyond more cedar breaks, lay miles of sand dunes.

"You suppose he could have doubled back and gone north along the cliffs?" Short asked.

"Not unless he knows another way through that wall," Hardin replied; "and if he did he left no tracks. I scouted for sign first thing after daybreak."

Neill waited, enjoying the warmth of the morning sun. He had slept badly, even tired as he was, for he had too few blankets for the cold night, and he kept worrying about his wife.

This was lonesome country. Since daybreak they had seen nothing that lived except a lone buzzard, prospecting them for future attention.

37

Kimmel drew up beside Neill and dug into his pocket for his plug tobacco, sized it up, and bit off a small chew. "Beats me," he said, "what a man would want to live in this country for. Especially if he's got a woman."

"She'll be Navajo," Short speculated. "He's got him a squaw."

To the frontier way of thinking, nobody was lower than a squawman ... and such men were not to be trusted. Not that anybody would trust a back-shooter, anyway.

Their suspicions had mounted as they rode north. They looked narrowly at the hills. It seemed unlikely that an honest man would hide out so far from other people.

"He might be a Mormon," McAlpin suggested. "Looks like he's ridin' right into Utah."

"If he is, we might as well turn ourselves right around and head for home. We'll be running right into a war. Anyway, ain't there some Mormon or other runnin' Lee's Ferry?"

"Was," Hardin agreed, "but I think he left the country. Too lonesome for him."

They waited upon the decision that would be made by Hardin and Chesney. Finally Hardin spoke. "Bill, we've got to gamble. We've got small chance to pick up that man's trail. I mean, he's like an Indian, and he knows this country. It might take us days to find it, even if we ever did. If he headed south into the sand dunes, we've lost him. There's stretches down there where the sand never stops moving, and the past couple of days there's been a wind—not much, but enough to cover any tracks."

"How do you mean ... gamble?"

"We've got to guess where he's headed for, and light out and run, try to beat him to it."

"And if we guess wrong?"

"Then we've lost him. We'll have to go back home and wait for him."

"Could be a damn' long wait," Kimmel replied. "I figure he kept on going northeast. If he was a Mormon he wouldn't have come south; he'd have gone north into Mormon country when he wanted supplies.

"And if he was a squawman he'd be apt to go east toward the New Mexican villages and the Santa Fe country. You take my word for it, that Key-Lock man lives right around here, right in this country. Although," he added grimly, "it's a damned big country!"

Bill Chesney made up his mind. "We'll head for the Crossin' of the Fathers. If he ain't there, or doesn't show up soon, we'll drop back downstream to Lee's Ferry. I can't see him in this country, Kim. He's a no-good drifter . . . a man would have to have sand in his craw to live around here."

"If he hadn't any when he got here," Neill commented, "he'd get it mighty soon by living here."

Chesney led off, circling back to a dim trail they had seen earlier, a trail passed by when they had seen no tracks.

Now their travel was swift. But when they reached the Crossing on the following day, they found no tracks there. Scouting upstream and down, they found much evidence of the high water resulting from a sudden rain several weeks back, but they found no tracks made since that time.

"We've lost him," McAlpin said. "He's got off, scot-free."

"Not by a damn' sight!" Chesney said. "He ain't never goin' to get off!"

"Well," Hardin said, "that may be so, Bill, and it may not. One thing I know: if we don't high-tail it down to Lee's Ferry and get us some grub we won't live long enough to find him."

"I'm for that," Short agreed.

So, though he grumbled, Chesney led the way south, in a line with the river, but back far enough from it to avoid its twisting course. Hardin glanced back at the looming bulk of Navajo Mountain. "From up there," he said, "a man could see just about all over this country."

The Key-Lock man, who lay flat on a rock near the crest of Navajo Mountain, trained his field glasses on the distant riders. One by one he counted them ... six men. It was the posse, all right, and they were heading south for Lee's Ferry. Undoubtedly they would buy supplies there; but how long could they remain away from their own crops, their own cattle?

He dared not watch them any longer. That they had lost his trail was obvious, and they would have trouble finding it, but he was overdue back home where Kristina waited for him, and she knew little of this land. He was a good thirty miles from there, by the way he must ride.

He went back down the steep, dangerous trail to War God Spring and refilled his canteen. Again he allowed his horse to drink.

Once off the mountain, he rode southeast along the plateau. It was good going for the first twelve miles, until he reached the breaks of Piute Mountain, and by that time the sun was painting the mountains with lavish reds and cresting the ridges with gold.

The big horse was weary, and he himself was as tired as man could be, but he pushed on through the rough country until he came to the fork of the trail. This was the way he had come, and it would be easier, although longer, to push on south. But he feared to leave tracks that searchers might find, so he swung again toward the north, and by moonrise he was skirting Tall Mountain.

Slowing to a walk, he looked for the turn-off that would take him along the canyon that cut deep into Skeleton Mesa. He could not go through—if a way existed, he had not found it—but must head the canyon and then double back.

Thinking of the trail off the mesa near the cliff

houses, he broke into a cold sweat. No doubt the trail had been a good one hundreds of years before when the mysterious Indians had used it, but erosion and slides had left it a chancy thing even by daylight.

The night was more than half gone when at last he drew rein at the lip of the cliff trail and felt the coolness rising from the pools below, and heard the distant sound of the waterfalls.

He put a gentle hand on the horse's neck. "That's home, boy. Right down there. You've got to be careful now."

Once, by daylight, he had taken the big horse up the trail, but never had he attempted to come down in the darkness. "All right, boy," he said at last, "just take your time."

The big horse tugged at the bit; he was worried yet eager. Tentatively, he put a hoof down the trail, snorted a time or two, and then delicately, as if walking on thin ice, he picked his way down the narrow trail. From time to time a rock rattled off down the cliff and fell among the rocks below.

By the night of the sixteenth day, Kristina rode her horse down the canyon to its junction with the main canyon and sat her horse there in the darkness, watching an occasional bat circling in the sky above, and listening for some sound.

He would come. Somehow, deep within her, she knew she was not deserted. Earlier there had been moments of doubt, but with the coming of darkness all her fears of being abandoned left her. If he had not come, it was because something had happened. Perhaps Neerland had found him.

She had little doubt now that Neerland would follow them, for he was a man to whom hate was a driving force. Hate was as necessary to Neerland as the blood that flowed in his veins. And somehow she was sure that when he came he would not come alone.

She had not been idle during this time, for being idle had never been her way. The life was new to her, but some of it was not entirely strange to her. She had hunted before this, and she had dressed game, so when she killed a deer she skinned it, dressed it, and cut some of the meat into strips for smoking. She had never done this before, but she had seen it done.

She had moved their things to a place under an overhang of the cliff, a place masked by willows and manzanita, and she had carefully made two beds of slender willow boughs and leaves. And then, she had moved the beds together, so that they were one bed.

The dwellers in the cliff houses had thrown their refuse over the edge and it had piled into a mound. She had climbed over this, looking at the odds and ends she found there, or the things she pushed out of the earth with a pointed stick.

There were fragments of pottery, some of it black and white, some orange, some red, and mixed with it were chunks of charcoal or discarded stone flakes chipped off in making arrowheads. There were bits of worn-out sandals, and broken knives of stone, and all these things gave her some idea of the people who had lived in this place. She wandered, too through the long-deserted rooms, trying to visualize the ones to whom this had been home.

Oddly enough, she was happy. The thought came to her suddenly on the fourth day of her being alone. She was alone, but her man was returning soon, and the solitude did not depress her. She had lived much among people, but she had loved the days on the high mountain slopes, loved the cold, icy solitudes, loved the dark forests. And just so she was coming to love this country.

Now that she looked about her, she realized that much of her life prepared her for this—skiing, climbing, riding, swimming . . . but with all these activities she had always returned to the high, lonely places in the mountains whenever possible.

Surprised as she was by the realization of her happiness, she was equally amused at the thought of what some of her friends might think if they could see her now. She, who had moved in court circles, happy and at home in this lonely canyon, far from the easy, gracious life she had known.

She discovered a small patch of level ground which was grown to grass and brush, but which could easily be cleared and planted. They would have a vegetable garden there. It was close beside the small stream, so there would be ample water. She had always loved gardening, although until now it had been a thing to do merely for pleasure; now it would be work that held meaning.

She found that she could not remain long away from the pile at the foot of the cliff. When she was a child, a frequent visitor in her home had been Christian Jurgensen Thomsen, the Danish archaeologist who had first divided pre-history into the ages of Stone, Bronze, and Iron. Many times he had taken her through his museum in Copenhagen, and she had seen its counterpart in Stockholm as well.

By family tradition as well as by training and education, her father had been a diplomat, but his preference was for study and research, and his home was a stopping place for most of the scholars of Europe. Both Boucher de Perthes and William Pengelly had visited her home, and had talked to her about the origins of prehistoric man.

Fascinated by these strange ruins here of which she had previously heard nothing, she collected hundreds of fragments of pottery, bits of sandals, arrowheads, and other evidence of the people long gone. But always in the back of her mind was the growing fear that something might have happened, that Matt had met Neerland again, or been killed by Indians, or been thrown from his horse.

But on the sixteenth night her doubts had somehow left her, and she knew he would come. Somewhere out there in the darkness he rode under these same stars, he smelled the desert as she was smelling it, he felt the coolness of the night.

At last she rode back, unsaddled her horse, and led him to water; then she picketed him on the grass nearby.

Hours later, she woke suddenly, hearing him nicker. Swiftly she rose from where she lay and took up the rifle Matt had left with her.

She listened for the sound of hoofs, and heard them at last, a walking horse, coming along surely and steadily. With her rifle in her hands she waited, her lips dry with excitement, her heart beating heavily.

And then she heard him speak. "All right, boy, we made it. We're home."

She sank down on her knees, trembling.

five

The Key-Lock man rode up Skeleton Mesa on a black horse. He rode to a high point east of a cliff dwelling and due north of Marsh Pass. Dismounting there, he climbed up the rocks to a slightly higher spot.

There was no actual peak here, but the place was high enough to allow him to look across the canyons and down the valley toward Castle Butte and the sand dunes. He had a fair sweep of country before him, and he sat down with his field glasses and waited.

It was not yet daylight, but what he hoped to catch was a drift of smoke or dust, or the glint of dawning light on metal. Or rather, it was what he hoped not to catch. He wanted to be left alone.

He remained right where he was for almost an hour, while the sun rose behind him and swept the shadows from the broad land. He saw the Echo Cliffs, many miles away, turn to gold; he saw the valley become white and still under the sun, and saw Thief

45

Rock standing straight and still and dark, as though no sun could reach it.

He saw a buzzard ... he saw a band of wild horses ... he saw a few quail nearby. But he saw no riders, nor any sign of human life. Not even an Indian.

As he watched he was thinking of Kristina. He perhaps had been a fool to bring her here, a fool to marry her. He only knew that from the moment he saw her he knew she was his woman, that she was born for him.

Kristina was better educated than he, and she had known well a world of which he knew little. She had, to be sure, climbed mountains in Europe, she had camped out, she had even roughed it on boats, but she had no idea what she faced here.

He was sure he loved her, and in her own way and her own time, she was coming to love him. But love was not enough. A marriage is as much a product of thoughtfulness and consideration as of love, and he was thinking now of what he must do. The primitive surroundings he could accept were not right for her. Nor was the life of the frontier quite what she would prefer, although she had accepted it and was adapting as if born to it. But he did not want to see her become toughened by work, by the sun and wind.

His thoughts veered. Neerland, he was sure, would come looking, and Neerland would not come alone. Moreover, his every instinct warned him that though he had been lucky with Neerland, he could not depend on luck again. For Neerland was a dangerous man, a man who knew how to hate; and he was no coward. . . . He might come at any time.

He relaxed, waited, and taking up the glasses once more, he saw again the band of wild horses, drifting restlessly through the scattered brush toward the water near Thief Rock. He had seen their tracks there, and he intended to look them over. Sometimes there were good horses among them, but the Navajos and Piutes had weeded them out, taking most of the good ones.

After some time he returned the glasses to the case and rode the horse down into the canyon. He was eager to be with Kristina, yet strangely reluctant too. As yet he knew so little about her, for she did not talk of herself—at least, she had not yet.

He saw the smoke rising from the fire, but it was a thin smoke . . . that she had learned quickly enough. Smoke could be either a warning or an invitation, and in this country where he had many enemies and no friends, the only kind of an invitation it could be was an invitation to trouble.

"Nothing," he said, in reply to her unspoken question. "I think they have gone back."

"Will they come again?"

He considered that, recalling the faces of the men as he had seen them when lying close behind the bank of the arroyo. "Yes . . . one of them, at least."

He had never known freedom from danger, never since he was a child, and he had grown accustomed to watchfulness. It was something that had ingrained itself deeply. It did not show, but it was there in all his actions, and he was forever alert.

She showed him her collection now, and he was fascinated. "In Europe they study things like this, and it is beginning to be a science. I knew a man . . ." She went on to tell him about Thomsen and the others and about some of the things they had told her as a child.

Then she continued: "There's a bit of ground over there where I thought we might plant some vegetables. The Indians grew corn, and some kind of melons or squash, so maybe we can."

They went down to the patch she spoke of. He took an axe along and began clearing the ground. The growth was sparse, just brush and canyon growth, and by late afternoon they had cleared a good little corner. The next day he dug it up, and she raked it over and planted some of the seed—corn, beans, peas, and pumpkins. By the end of a week, they had cleared and planted half an acre.

By this time the supplies he had been forced to abandon in Freedom were desperately needed, yet he held back, reluctant to ride away again. Meanwhile he rode, at least twice a day, to the lookout points on the hills around.

Oskar Neerland was standing on the street when the posse rode in, and he watched them as they swung down tiredly from their horses and trooped into the saloon for a drink.

Sam took a bottle from the back bar and placed it out for them. He needed to ask no questions.

"Lost him," Chesney said. "He just dropped off the edge of the world."

"He'll be back," Kimmel said. "That man needed grub. He rode out of here with nothing, nothing but a woman's comb."

Neerland had followed them in, and he was leaning on the bar, not looking at them, but listening. He had trailed the Key-Lock man this far, and he had listened to talk of the shooting, and to descriptions of the man who had killed Johnny.

"Know where we lost him?" McAlpin said. Short looked up at the words. "At Mormon Well!"

Sam was polishing a glass, but his hand froze. "*Mormon Well?*"

"Uh-huh." McAlpin could not hold back the story. "Led us right to it, then just clean dropped out of sight."

"You talk too damn' much," Short growled.

Sam rested his hands on the bar. "Mormon Well—that's the key to the Lost Wagons. Why, you could be rich men! When you goin' back?"

"Well, now . . ." McAlpin put his glass down. "Seems to me—"

"You let him get away, then," Neerland interrupted.

Their eyes turned to him, a stranger, and their faces were blank, noncommittal. Except for Chesney.

"Not by a damned sight!" he said in an ugly tone. "I'll follow him to hell, if need be."

"You've all got outfits that need care and attention," Neerland suggested. "Me, I'm footloose."

"What's that mean?" Chesney demanded.

"It's cheaper to hire somebody to hunt that killer. You men could work your ranches, let me do the hunting. I'll find him. In fact, I know who he is."

"You know him?"

"Uh-huh—his name is Matt Keelock. That's why he uses that brand."

"We won't need any help," Hardin said. "We'll find him."

"My name's Oskar Neerland, and I've come west hunting a place to light." He waved a hand. "Seems like a nice town here, and I'm favorable to taking this chore off your hands. Of course, I'd want some sort of right."

"Right?"

"Well, I don't want to just start hunting a man, not just off-hand. I'd want the *right* to hunt him, like as if I was marshal."

It was a new idea, and their faces showed it. Hardin started to speak, then held his peace. Bill Chesney was saying nothing. The others waited, looking to Chesney or Hardin for a lead.

"We've had no trouble here," Hardin said. "I don't think there's any need for a town marshal."

Neill had not spoken. He wanted nothing so much as to get back to his wife and his ranch and stay there. Right at the moment he did not care if he ever left it again, and the idea of having the pursuit taken off their hands was appealing. At the same time, he did not trust this cold-looking stranger—he did not trust him at all. And he had a feeling that Hardin felt the same way.

"There'd have to be a town meeting," Chesney said after a moment; "we're just a few." Sam looked at him in surprise, as did Neill. Hardin was obviously not at all surprised. "I mean," Chesney went on, "there's others to vote besides us."

"I'll be around." Neerland tossed off his drink and put the glass down on the bar. "I'm camped over by the creek."

He walked out, and the wings of the door fanned themselves shut. The room remained silent behind him until Neill said, "I've got to get home. My wife will be worried."

"Me, too," Hardin said.

Chesney straightened up. "Well, why not? Why not hire this man? We could go back to our places and let him carry on ... only I want in on the hanging when we take him. Let this man find him, then we can all move in and make it official."

"We don't know him, Bill," Hardin suggested. "We don't know who or what he is."

"Aw, hell!" Short said, "we can always call a town meeting and throw him out. Just because we hire him, we don't have to keep him. Fact is, I don't think he'd stay on. He just wants the job long enough to find this man."

"How do you figure that?"

"Look at it. He knew who we were talkin' about, even knew the man's name. I'd guess he rode in here huntin' him."

"Then why pay him?" Hardin said. "Come on, Neill. I'm riding your way."

Chesney threw a hard look at them as they started for the door. "You mean you're against it, Hardin? You're against hirin' this man?"

Hardin stopped, considered the matter for a long, slow minute, and then he said quietly, "Yes, Bill, I am

against it. I don't like the man, and I don't trust him.
I say we scotch our own snakes."

Deliberately, Chesney turned his back on them,
and after a moment they walked out.

At the hitch rail Neill tightened his girth. "I don't
know what to make of Bill," he said. "He's changed."

"He'll be all right, kid. He's just tired and sore, like
all of us."

Yet Neill was sure that Hardin was worried. Chesney *was* different. He was sour, bitter. He had always
been a hard man, but with a certain tough, genial
humor that was no longer there. Neill had always
respected Bill Chesney, and admired him, too. But he
had always been a little uneasy around him, watchful
for fear he would say or do the wrong thing. A man
had a feeling about Bill Chesney, a feeling that there
was little leeway in him. He was a man who was
utterly sure of his own rightness ... not that he was
cocky or assertive, simply that once he had made a
decision he could not conceive of there being any
other way that could be right.

Oskar Neerland, in his camp by the river, watched
them ride out of town, and smiled after them. It was
not a nice smile.

He knew the opposition when he saw it, and knew
what a mistake they had made. They felt by riding
out they would break up the meeting, put an end to
the whole idea ... at least, the older one would think
that.

Usually when one man made a move, such a
gathering broke up, and all of these men were tired
and ready to ride home. Neerland, with a quick grasp
of the situation, had rightly judged the man who
counted was Chesney. Hardin was easy-going, and
perhaps the brightest of the lot; but the very fact that
he was intelligent would tend to make him a middle-
of-the-roader. Chesney, on the other hand, was of the
stuff that fanatics are made of. Short and McAlpin—

he had learned all their names before ever returning—
would follow Chesney's lead.

Kimmel ... he was the doubtful one. A solid, tough
man. In a last-ditch fight, Kimmel would be there,
among the fighters. Oskar Neerland decided to avoid
any contact with Kimmel, to side-step any issue on
which Kimmel might oppose him. Sometimes the best
way of eliminating a fighter was by simply not
providing the chance for him to fight. Neerland could
handle the tough ones when he had to, but in the
meantime it was best to circle away from them, giving them no grounds for opposition.

He went over to the fire. His coffee water was
boiling.

He dumped in the coffee and waited, still thought-
ful. He was going to snare two birds in the same trap.
He was going to wipe out his score with the Key-Lock
man, and he was going to take this town and wrap it
up. There was not much to be had here, but enough
to make it worthwhile, and it would be like taking
candy from a baby. And then he would ride on west
with that blonde and a good big stake to start him out
somewhere else. From the hour when he rode into
Freedom he had known what he was going to do.

There was no finesse about Oskar Neerland. He had
no involved or complicated plan, for the simple reason that he was not a complicated man. He was big,
tough, and brutal ... and completely devoid of any
feeling for the rights of others.

Now he dropped some cold water in the pot to
settle the grounds, and never gave a thought to Neill.

Nor did he consider Kristina, beyond what he
planned to do to her. Had he been able to raise the
spirits of the dead, he might have had good advice
from a certain Austrian military attaché, who had
also misunderstood Kristina.

six

Matt Keelock was a man with a lot of hopes and few illusions. He had a clear and definite idea of what he wanted from life. At least, he knew what he wanted *first*.

He wanted a ranch with good grass and water, and he wanted cattle to make money, and horses simply because he loved them. He was not waiting around to fall heir to a fortune, nor to marry a rich wife, nor to steal enough to get by. He knew there was no easy way, and he was not looking for one. It was his pride that he walked his own trail, saddled his own broncs, and fought his own battles. And he earned his own money.

That he faced a fight now, a fight that might come at him from several directions, was a fact he understood and accepted. If they wanted his kind of trouble, they could have it. He had measured himself against the land and against other men, and he stood prepared to give as good as he got, and a little more.

53

Kristina had been unexpected. In the back of his mind there had been a picture of the woman he wanted, a woman to walk beside him, not behind him. The face was indistinct, but the character was not. He knew the life he planned to lead would not be easy, and he knew what manner of woman was needed for it. When he saw Kristina he knew she was the one.

He had planned the home he would take her to, this girl of whom he had dreamed, but now that he found her he had no such home for her. He had only a rock overhang near a pool of water in a raw, harsh land.

Each day he spent here on the mountain was a day of searching, not only searching the country for the approach of enemies, but searching his own mind for a plan of action.

A man needed a plan, he needed direction. If he did not have that, he had nothing. A man, like a ship at sea, might change course many times in getting to an eventual destination, but he must always be going somewhere, not simply drifting.

Matt Keelock did not plan to remain in Navajo country. The area he favored was south and west, in the timbered country of the White Mountains and west of them. But he had known of a band of wild horses running in the breaks of the Colorado, and he wanted these. He had seen them once, and among them a colt.

The Navajos or Utes might have captured them by now, but he did not think so. Even the Indians who came into this far and lonely land were few. With any luck, he would ride away from here with some fine breeding stock.

Most wild horses weren't of much account, but among the thousands that ran on the plains and in the mountains, there were many splendid creatures. Time and careless breeding would change them, the best would be captured, the breeding would become less good, and before many years they would be scrubs. But for the present this was not so.

This particular bunch of horses had a particular origin, however, and a reason for being the stock they were. And he knew about where to look for them. Tomorrow they would ride north toward the river, and try to locate the herd.

The worst of it was, he desperately needed supplies. When he had raced away from Freedom ahead of a hanging posse, he had left behind the supplies he had ridden so far to get.

They needed meat too, and there was a good chance that they might kill a bighorn or a deer on their trip tomorrow.

Kristina waited for him by the pool. "I have fixed our supper," she said; but neither of them moved. The sun was setting in the red gorge and the walls were like living flame. They stood there watching the light change, listening to the quail calling mournfully, and hearing the replies.

"I love the stillness," she said. "Somehow it seems to soak through me, smoothing out all the rough places, making all my troubles seem as nothing."

When they ate their supper it was in near silence. They talked a little of commonplace things, each alive to the presence of the other.

Before turning in, he made a last stroll around, walking to the corral—merely a brush corral with a rope strung from tree to tree. The buckskin, already rested, nickered and plucked at his sleeve.

Their camp was well hidden. For anyone riding by way of Marsh Pass—and not many did—there was no reason to turn off and ride up the canyon. The entrance was wide, but promised nothing, while Marsh Pass opened ahead and seemed to draw one on.

He glanced toward the great open-faced cavern that sheltered the mysterious ruins. The bulge of the cliff face above them was streaked with dark stains left by unnumbered ages of rain. The great ruins lay ghostlike and still, dwarfed by the immensity of the cavern and the towering cliff above.

This was a good place, and he would regret leaving it. There were ghosts here, he felt, but he could not disturb them, and they seemed to know that his way was their way also, as if they could sense his love for the silent land.

Kristina came quietly and stood beside him in the stillness.

"After all you have known, this must seem another world," he said.

"I am glad that it is, Matt, but somehow when I look out there now it is hard for me to believe I ever knew any other. My people were a mountain people in their time, and we take naturally to the wilderness."

In the morning, by way of a devious trail masked by brush and the fallen rocks below the cliffs, they rode out of the canyon and headed north. Twice, far off, Keelock saw antelope. A jack-rabbit leaped from under his horse's hoofs and sprang away, and he timed its third jump and got it with a bullet from his Colt.

"A man can starve to death eating rabbits," he commented, "but we'll have this much meat at least."

Twice he saw the tracks of wild horses, and studied them with care. Once they followed the tracks for several miles, but when the horses drifted down a trail into the deeper canyons, he let them go.

"The band I want runs further north," he said. "We will ride on."

They were skirting the base of Boot Mesa when they saw the horses at last. The band had come down the canyon of Moonlight Creek and out on the flatland, where they walked slowly along, grazing from the brush and grass as they moved.

Several minutes passed before they saw the golden stallion. He had topped out and was standing motionless on a knoll, head up, ears pricked.

They were more than a mile off, but the air was clear and his glasses brought the horses close. "He's the color of a gold coin," Matt said, "and there seems to be a splash of white over the rump. I think this is the band that I want."

He turned the glasses to examine the other horses. There were twenty-five to thirty head, most of them mares, and several of them had splashes of white over the shoulders or rump. He could not see if they were otherwise marked.

He passed the glasses to Kristina. "Look at the stallion. I want him, and some of the others."

"There was a Mormon came into this country a few years back," he went on, "and he brought some of the finest horses you've ever seen. His name was Ed Linnett, and his father came west with the original stock from Virginia and Kentucky. Then Ed picked up a fine stallion and some mares from the Nez Percés up in Idaho."

"Aren't these wild horses?"

"You bet they are—wild as they come. Ed came out on the wrong end of a fight with a grizzly. He was hunting a colt one of the mares had hidden and he found it the same time this she grizzly did. He wounded the bear and it charged him. He killed the bear, but it killed him, too."

"He must have been quite a man."

"He was all of that, and he never weighed over a hundred and thirty pounds, soaking wet. When that grizzly tackled that colt of his, he tackled Ed Linnett. Ed was all torn up by grizzly teeth and claws, but that bear had nine or ten stab marks in its hide where Ed got home with his hunting knife. Ed never did take to anything worrying his stock."

They rode along a wash that would intersect the one followed by the wild horses, going warily so as not to come suddenly upon the herd. And Matt Keelock was careful, even now, to check his back trail. Long ago he had learned the way to survive was to watch your back trail and keep a gun handy.

He did not plan to try catching the golden stallion now. He only wanted to estimate the limits of its range, to find out its watering holes and its favorite grazing places. Most of all, he wanted the horses to become familiar with him, to get the idea that his presence did not imply danger.

Twice, just before sundown, they were within half a mile or less, but each time they veered off, giving the stallion ample time to see them, and to know that he was seen. Head up, nostrils distended, he watched them as they rode by the last time, only a few hundred yards off.

That night they camped in a cove of Hoskinini Mesa, their fire hidden from observation by the cove and its brush and boulders.

During the night they heard the horses pass, pause in their passing to test the man smell, then walk on. One horse lingered after the others.

"Now that one," Matt said in a low voice, "that one might be a horse that's just gone wild. Could be it remembers the smell of man and of woodsmoke."

Long after Kristina slept, Matt lay awake, looking up at the stars and thinking about the posse. They had been determined men, pursuing him for what they believed was rightful cause, and they would not soon give up. He fell asleep wondering what the next move would be.

Nobody in Freedom or the country around wanted to make an enemy of Bill Chesney. They respected him for his energy, his honesty and courage, but were also aware that he was a hard man and an impatient one. He entered into everything with drive and purpose, and whatever needed to be done was done without delay if he had anything to do with it.

Consequently, when Chesney came into the saloon the next morning, shortly after opening time, Sam was wary. Sam had tended bar and operated saloons long enough to know the smell of trouble, and he had caught the scent of it the night before.

"Neerland been around?" Chesney asked.

"Leave him alone, Bill. He's trouble with a capital T."

Chesney threw him a hard look. "He's trouble for that Key-Lock man."

"Maybe . . . and maybe for us."

Chesney ignored this. He had made up his mind and was not to be disputed. "You don't have to like him. I ain't seen that he's runnin' for any popularity contests."

"You puttin' him up for town marshal?"

"He wants it like that. If he catches that man I don't care what he calls himself."

"I don't like it, Bill."

Chesney looked at him irritably. "Maybe it just don't matter what you like! You want to go chase him yourself?"

Sam's lips tightened, and abruptly he turned his back on Chesney. Yet a man had to make allowances. After all, Johnny had been Chesney's friend, and a friend counted for something in this country.

Taplinger came in, and after him, George Benson, and the two of them sat down at a table. Neither man spent much time around the saloon, and Sam had a good idea why they had come now. Chesney turned away from the bar and carried his drink to their table.

Taplinger had built a house on the edge of town and had a few cattle running on the hills nearby. He talked of building a sawmill, but so far it had been just talk. George Benson was a partner in the general store, a self-important man who talked politics and let it be known that he had held office back east.

Sam carried their drinks to the table and returned to the bar to pick up the glass he had been polishing. Mitchell would be the next one . . . and then they would start talking about a town marshal. He glanced out the window and down the narrow, dusty lane that led toward Hardin's place. Now, why the hell wasn't Hardin here? If ever the town of Freedom needed his quiet way and his brains, it was now.

"Of course, we need a marshal," Taplinger was saying. "There's too many trouble-makers adrift these days. Look at that man who did the shooting the other day. Just a no-account drifter."

"I'm not too positive about that." Benson took the cigar from his teeth. "Over at the store they said he ordered a big lot of supplies . . . a big lot."

Taplinger laughed. "George, you know better than that. Another minute or two and he'd have been asking credit. We have had too many of that kind around. It wouldn't be as if he owned something about the country."

Joe Mitchell came in and went to their table. He ordered a beer and leaned his skinny forearms on the table. "That there man of yours, Chesney. You reckon he's right for the job?"

Chesney glanced at him. "He's asked for it. He sizes up like a tough man in any crowd."

Sam put a glass on the back bar, and looked out the window and down the street. Where was Hardin? Or even Neill. Neill didn't stampede, he would say that for him, and he had a way of resisting without making an issue of it.

John Ware was out of town, over at Prescott, and John would not stand for this, Sam was thinking, not for a minute. It was a foolish thing to do . . . there had been no trouble here the townspeople couldn't handle.

Only occasionally could Sam hear a word, but he could guess at those he did not hear. Well, he might make an enemy of Bill Chesney and he certainly would make one of Neerland, but he was going to cast his vote against it. The worst of it was, according to the town laws they had drawn up, only a third of the property owners need be present to vote on any issue affecting the town itself, and that meant just twelve men were needed to appoint a marshal. And with Taplinger, Chesney, Mitchell, and Benson to head the list, the others could be found.

Short and McAlpin came into the saloon then and went to the bar. Chesney called to them.

"Later," Short said. He looked over at Sam. "Give me that bottle."

Sam pushed the bottle and two glasses over the bar. He nodded toward the table. "I don't like that deal. I don't like it a damn' bit."

Short shrugged. "What the hell? It's no skin off your nose."

Taking the bottle, he went with McAlpin to another table. Sam saw Short drawing a design upon the table-top. He held a pencil in his fingers, and he was making an X. "Now right there," he was saying, "is Mormon Well. If we ..." Short's voice lowered and Sam could hear no more. Nor did he need to hear more. It was the Lost Wagons again.

Chesney came over to the table. "Damn it, Short!" he said. "I want to talk to you, I want—"

"I know what you want. You want to make Neerland town marshal and let him go man-hunting. All right, you've got my vote."

"Mine, too," McAlpin said.

Chesney turned on his heel and went back to his own table. Sam had listened and heard. . . . Where the devil was Hardin?

seven

Matt Keelock made his plans with care. He wanted that golden stallion and he wanted some of the mares, so he held aloof, letting them become used to his presence, and he studied their grazing and watering habits. Within a week he knew the track of each of the herd. He had killed an antelope on the first day, a deer on the fourth.

He and Kristina were never apart. She rode beside him, hunted beside him. The whiteness left her skin and it became brown under the wind and the sun. The wilderness began to give her its awareness; she began to feel that its stillness was a part of her. Far, far behind her now were the places in Europe that she had known. She scarcely thought of them any more, so demanding and so exciting was the day-to-day living.

On the tenth day, their coffee gone, they rode back to the camp in the canyon near the great ruin.

For a long time Keelock studied the place before

they approached it. He skirted the cliffs, looking down into the basin from every aspect, searching for anyone who might have hidden near by. Only after some hours did he descend into the canyon, and then he went alone.

They packed their things, and after that was done he left the pack animals and rode alone to the mouth of the canyon. Where it opened into Marsh Pass he dismounted, changed to moccasins, and walked down to the trail to check on the travel.

The tracks were few, mostly those of Indian ponies or wild horses, and he had turned to go back when he saw a boot print, the mark of a large, heavy man. Near by were the hoof marks of a shod horse ... a freshly shod one.

The traveler had paused there, dismounted, waiting and no doubt listening. He had then ridden on along Marsh Pass.

Keelock had never seen Neerland's tracks, but he had a feeling these were his. The weight and height were about right—the man's height estimated by the length of his stride. When Matt returned to his horse he walked on rocks, careful to leave no tracks behind.

Kristina was standing waiting when he came up the trail. She came to him quickly.

"Out there," he gestured, "I saw some tracks. I think they belong to Oskar Neerland."

"Will he find us?"

Keelock shrugged. "Maybe he'll find the camp. There's too much sign there. But he won't find our trail out of it, not unless he's a tracker of ghosts. I fixed the lower part of the trail, made a blind over the approach ... it looks as if it's been undisturbed for years. And there's no way to leave a track on the rock of the trail itself."

They rode steadily north until they were back in the domain of the golden stallion, and they camped that night on Moonlight Creek near the point of rocks. Those rocks, in a vast jumble, stretched away to the north, to the San Juan and beyond. Westward the land was gathering shadows as they built their fire.

Taking her arm, Matt pointed to the west where, a dozen miles away, a vast bulk blocked off their horizon. "No Man's Mesa," he said. "The highest part is a good thousand feet above the country around, and the cliffs are nowhere less than five hundred feet high.

"It's all of nine miles long, and from a quarter of a mile to a mile and a half wide on top. They call it No Man's Mesa because there's supposed to be no way to the top. I think there *is* a way. If we get separated, you go to the western side. A bit over two-thirds of the way along there's a place I want to try. Stop where the cliff curves away toward the east. I'll meet you there."

The next morning they saw the stallion, saw him suddenly, and close up.

They were riding westward, passing Organ Rock, when the stallion emerged from a draw and scrambled up the bank. He stopped, head up, nostrils distended, not fifty yards away. Had they been out on a flat, or at least on good ground, Matt might have tried to make a catch right there. A quick run and a good cast of the rope and he might have him. On the other hand, the slope was soft sand and the ground bad for running. His horse might break a leg, and if he failed to make his catch, all the work leading up to this would be lost.

The sheer magnificence of the stallion arrested him. At close range he was even more splendid than at a distance. He was the color of a bright gold coin with a splash of white across the hips, the white flecked with spots of gold. He had a white nose and three white anklets. His neck was arched, his head held proudly.

He stood, ears up, looking at Matt and Kristina. His

mares, following swiftly, came up out of the draw and drew up around him.

For just an instant the tableau held. "Hello, boy," Matt said. "Want to make friends?"

The horse tossed his head, and then with a snort, led the way by a devious path through the rocks and into the open again, the mares trailing close behind. Of the other horses following, several were young stallions, but whether mares or stallions, they were fine stock. The stallions, Matt noticed, trailed at a respectful distance.

As they disappeared into the flatland below, Matt glanced at Kristina. "What do you think?" he said. "Is it worth it?"

"It is," Kristina answered softly, "it really is! Oh, Matt, isn't he wonderful!"

Together, they trailed along behind the horses, moving at a fast walk.

"Kris," Matt said, "there's a story about some lost wagons in this country, and all the gold they are supposed to contain. Well, they can have it. All I want is that stallion and a couple of those mares."

He drew up suddenly, sharply, swinging his horse to stop hers from moving further. Her eyes, already accustomed to looking for trail sign, followed his.

In front of them, partly obliterated by the passage of the wild herd, were the tracks of three shod horses, and they were fresh tracks.

"Made last night," he said. "Kris, we've got to get under cover."

Wheeling his buckskin, he rode back along the trail made by the mustangs as they left the draw. He back-trailed them swiftly, following the draw, with Kris and the pack mules close behind.

The followed the trail back, then cut off and rode westward along the base of Hoskinini Mesa and into the mouth of Copper Canyon. Turning there, they looked back, but there was no dust, no evidence of movement in all the wide country that lay there in their view.

"Three men," he said, "on freshly shod horses."

"Are they looking for us?"

He shrugged. "Maybe."

For a long while they watched the plain, and then, riding up Copper Canyon, Matt cut off to the westward. By early afternoon they had made camp in Cattle Canyon under the towering rim of Piute Mesa.

Over a small fire, in a sheltered place among the rocks and brush, Kristina broiled venison while he rubbed down their horses and scouted the country around them.

"Matt, tell me about the Lost Wagons," she said when they were ready to eat.

"All right." But what he said then was, "Kris, I think one of those men made the same tracks I saw in Marsh Pass. We've got to hole up somewhere and wait it out."

"We haven't much to eat."

"No ... can you stick it?"

She smiled. "Of course, Matt. As long as you can."

When they had eaten they put out the fire and drew back into a thick nest of rocks to which there was no easy approach. In a hollow, they picketed their horses.

"About Lost Wagons," he said when they had settled down. "It's an old story. The West is filled with buried treasure of one kind or another, and some of it has been found. In any country where there is danger, as from the Indians, or where folks have to travel light and fast, they are apt to bury gold or whatever they treasure. Sometimes the owners get killed, and sometimes they lose their nerve. Gold can look almighty nice, but a few hundred miles of sun-blistered desert full of Apaches can look mean enough to take the shine off the gold.

"There were seventeen men started out of California with two carts and six mules to each cart, which was a-plenty. All seventeen had saddle horses, and all were seasoned, well-armed men. In the carts, aside from provisions of one sort or another, they had a lot of gold.

"How much? Well, it was enough. Nobody rightly knows now how much it was, because those stories grow mighty fast. The gold was in bars, and there were several sacks of nuggets, and of Spanish and French coins.

"They lost a man near the Colorado. Mohaves killed him. Somewhere near what is now Beale Springs another one died. He'd been poorly, and he caught an arrow in the fight near the Colorado, but nobody expected him to die.

"They could see San Francisco peaks off to the northeast, and were getting set to bed for the night when a party of Coyotero Apaches closed in on them. It was a three-day fight, and the whites lost another man and had a couple wounded, but not bad.

"That night one of the wounded men died, and nobody expected him to go, either. By now they were getting worried. They had some bad country ahead and they needed every man; but what worried them most was those two men dying, unexpectedly, like that. There just didn't seem any way to account for it, and they were getting superstitious.

"With just thirteen men left, hampered by the slow movements of the carts, they were in trouble, and they knew it. The other wounded man was well enough to ride, although he was carrying one arm in a sling. But he was a scared man, Kris. Two wounded men had died, and he was scared . . . and he had a right to be.

"Three good days of travel they had, without incident, and then that other wounded man died during the night. One of the party, a Frenchman named Valadon, was keeping a journal, and when he was fixing to bury the body he noticed a tiny spot of blood in one ear. He touched it, and found the end of a wire, like. Somebody had murdered that wounded man by pushing a needle-like piece of steel through his brain. Inside his ear like that, it could have gone unnoticed. So far as Valadon was concerned, that accounted for the deaths of the others, too. And it was being done by somebody in the company."

"How long ago was this, Matt?"

"Fifteen—maybe sixteen years ago. That's a long time, out here. Anyway, Valadon was scared, and he said as much in that journal. The murderer could be any one of them, and of course, nobody had to look for a motive. It was the gold.

"He told them at the fire that night. He laid it out before them all, telling them one of them was a murderer. The next morning, they went on, but by that time nobody trusted anyone else.

"Valadon and another man were scouting ahead when they saw the Coyoteros. They were some distance off, and there was a large party. He didn't know if they had been seen, so they slipped away quickly to warn the others.

"They decided to take a dim trail that led off to the northeast, and for the time being they lost the Apaches, who had probably not seen them, anyway. They also lost the gold.

"The trouble began with a sand storm in which they lost the trail they had been following. A mule broke a leg on the rocks, and they had to kill him. They fought and struggled and worked their way on toward the east, and then they found Mormon Well.

"It wasn't called that then . . . if it had any name it was some Indian name, but they only knew it was water, and enough water. But that night one of the men disappeared. He went out to the edge of camp after some fuel and it was some time before anybody realized he hadn't come back.

"Nobody ever saw him again. They found some tracks, but the trail just petered out near some rocks."

Keelock paused to listen to the night, his ears sorting the sounds.

"Eleven men left, and they were lost in a wilderness of rocks and canyons. They tried several ways through, but each time they ran into a dead-end canyon and had to back-track. With the wagons, that was a mean job. And then they lost another mule.

"Tempers were short, and several times they came near to fights. There was a youngster with them, fourteen or fifteen years old. He'd latched onto them before they left California, wanting to work his way east, and it was he who found the way through. It was a high, narrow pass that opened out into desert, but they made it through to the desert and then turned south along the mountains, following a dim Indian trail.

"Nobody knows how far they had gone when the Coyoteros hit them, but it was a complete surprise. One man fell in the first fire, and then they dropped behind rocks and fought back. The Indians ran off most of their stock, and when the fight was over there were just four men left, four men and that youngster.

"One of the men left alive was Valadon, and that was a fortunate thing, because he had kept the account of the trip. After the big fight there was almost another one among themselves, for Trim Newhall, one of the men, wanted to kill that youngster, the one they called Muley. It was all the others could do to stop him."

"But why, Matt?"

"Because when the fight with the Indians started the kid dug out and hid . . . he never helped one little bit."

"But he was just a boy!"

"In this country boys of that age usually do a man's work, and if they travel with men, they share alike in fighting or any other trouble. Valadon and Camp Foster managed to talk Newhall out of it, because they needed all the help they could get.

"With most of their stock gone, they had to abandon the wagons, so they loaded the gold on the mules and horses, and trailed them back into the rugged hills.

"They could not have gone far, for they were in a hurry. The Indians might return at any moment, and they were too few to resist an attack. So they hid the gold, returned to their cache of supplies near the wagons, and then headed south.

"Trim Newhall, Camp Foster, a man named Ben Hollenbeck, and that kid ... aside from Valadon they were the only ones left. . . . Nobody ever called the kid by any name other than Muley.

"They had kept enough gold to pay their way, and to outfit and return for the rest of it, and as you can imagine, it was a-plenty. Twelve men gone of the original lot, and gold enough hidden away to make those who remained rich men. Only there was a joker in the deck for Muley. Before the others hid the gold they tied him up and left him behind; then after they'd hidden it, they returned for him. After all, he'd no share in it.

"Yet one among them had murdered at least two, and perhaps three of the others. Was he among those killed? Or was he still one of those living?

"They rode together and they rode hard, and they switched horses from time to time. It was a brutal ride, but they got through to Santa Fe. They split up there, for no one of them trusted the others, but the following morning Valadon and Foster together went looking for Trim Newhall. They found him ... with a knife thrust in the ribs.

"They had been planning an immediate return for the gold, but Valadon had had enough. He slipped away, got his gear together, and before sundown had ridden out of town, en route for Las Vegas and then for St. Louis. He never returned, and he heard nothing of the others after that."

"But surely they went back for the gold?"

"Maybe. Of course, no treasure-hunter wants to believe they got it, and in this case there is good reason for not believing it.

"Actually, but for Valadon's journal nobody would have known of the lost wagons, for so far as could be discovered the others were also killed."

"All of them?"

He took his pipe from his pocket and tamped it full before replying. "All of them. All but Muley."

"Did they ever discover who did it?"

"No."

"Matt, let's look for it! You know this country. Maybe we could find it!"

"Honey, that stallion I'm chasing looks better to me than that gold, and in the long run, might be worth more. And don't you get started on that. Too many have died looking for that gold."

"Wasn't it buried near here?"

He listened into the night before replying. It was a way he had, and she did not hurry him. She also noticed that he watched the horses continually, observing their every reaction, for they might hear something approaching before he did.

"Gay Cooley hunted for that gold and never found it and he knew more about it than anyone. When Valadon died, the journal fell into the hands of his nephew, who came hunting it. Gay went with him."

"They couldn't find it?"

"They found a bunch of Piutes. A war party came down the Dirty Devil and crossed the Colorado at the Crossing of the Fathers. They wounded Valadon's nephew, scratched Gay a couple of times, and ran off their horses.

"It took Gay and that nephew a couple of months to get a decent meal, and by that time the nephew had had it. He simply took off for the East and left the journal with Gay. Aside from Gay, I'm the only man west of the Mississippi who ever saw that journal."

He rose and went down through the brush to listen.

She could never understand how he moved through the brush without a sound, but he did.

For some time he simply stood there alone, listening. As he listened, his mind reviewed their situation.

The posse from Freedom would not give up. He had seen their faces, and there were driving men in that lot. He had them to consider, as well as Neerland and whoever might be with him, and there was a good chance the two parties might find common cause. It was a big country, but not big enough if they really kept looking for him.

Deliberately, he had led them to Mormon Well, hoping their lust for gold would start them looking for it, but so far as the evidence indicated, the ruse had not worked.

He needed that stallion and some of the mares, and he had a feeling he could get them if time allowed. He needed time to locate their water holes, to find the best place to trap the herd. He needed thirty to forty days without interruption . . . and perhaps longer.

So what he needed was a delaying action, something to cause them to believe that he had left the country.

And he had an idea how it could be done.

eight

Until now he had deliberately put aside all thought of the trading post at Tuba City. It was nearer than any other, much nearer even than the tiny settlement of Freedom, but to ride into Tuba City was enough to put the news of his presence on the grapevine. Within a short time after he arrived, the news would have reached the farthest corner of northeastern Arizona.

And that was exactly what he wanted now.

"We'll pack up," he told Kris, "and we'll ride out of the country, heading for Prescott."

At her inquiring glance he added, "At least, we will make it look that way. We'll point for Prescott, and lay a fair set of tracks southwest until we can swing around through the sand hills where we'll leave no trail."

"You want them to think we've gone?"

"All we can lose is time."

"Suppose they are at this Tuba City place?"

There was that, of course; and if they were there

the showdown would come there and then. So be it.

There are tides in the affairs of men, tides of restlessness and awareness; there are thin threads of thought that reach out across the distance and, like the threads of a weaver, are drawn together tight. In his faraway ranch-house bed, Bill Chesney awoke suddenly, and lay there, hands clasped behind his head, staring up into the darkness.

Neerland was up there, but he'd be damned if he would leave the job to him. Tomorrow ... Kimmel was fancy-free again, and he would get Neill.

He hesitated over the name. Neill had irritated him a little with his occasional flippant remarks, and then toward the end there had been his seeming unwillingness to go along. The hell with him. . . . Still, Neill was a solid man, a good man.

His thoughts veered off to the north again. Tuba City ... he would ride north to Tuba City, and if there was anyone in the Navajo country, it would be known there. Sooner or later the Key-Lock man would have to come out for supplies, and Tuba City was the closest place. What they should have done was ride back there and just wait.

Though it was dark, he rolled out of bed and got into his clothes. He stirred up the fire and lighted a candle. Then he got his Winchester down and began to oil it. The firelight flickered on his hard-drawn features as his hands worked knowingly over the weapon.

At this hour, far to the north, where the hills made a cove of rocks, a campfire flickered. Oskar Neerland sat beside it, hunched in thought. He glanced over at the two men. Mitch was asleep, but the other one was still awake.

"We'll ride back to Tuba," Neerland said. "We'll start at sunup."

"All right." The rider was a lean-faced young man with bright blue eyes. "We catch them two," he said, "who gets the woman?"

Neerland turned his big head slowly around. His eyes leveled at the other man, cold and steady. "I do," he said. "I get her, and when I'm through, you can have her if you like. After I'm through with her, only one thing matters. She never leaves us alive."

The younger man shrugged. "Suits me," he said. He walked away from the fire and stood still, looking off into the darkness. That needle-rock off to the north, now . . .

He glanced back at Neerland, stirring the fire. He gave no thought to Neerland. The big man had motives of his own, and they were of no interest to him. He felt no loyalty, nor need for any. He had his own plans and his own ideas.

Neerland stepped out into the darkness. "I'm turning in. Check the horses, will you, Muley?"

Tuba City was an adobe trading post and a couple of uninhabited hogans that had been built by nomad Navajos. The place was named for a Hopi chief who had been guide to the Mormon, Jacob Hamlin, when he explored the region.

Matt Keelock slipped the rawhide thong from the hammer of his six-shooter and freed the Winchester in its scabbard for easy use, if need be.

They approached the post from the sand hills to the north, circled to the west, and studied the situation with care. Only one tired, crow-bait of an Indian pony stood at the hitch rail. All was quiet. It was early morning and a slow smoke lifted from the chimney of the trading post.

Inside, it was shadowed and cool. The adobe walls kept the coolness in and the heat of the sun out. A tall lanky man with a cowlick of hair over his forehead sat on the counter plaiting a rawhide belt. In a chair beside the unused stove, sat a stocky, muscular man, feet propped up. He had a hard brown face marked by a deep line, like a scar, down each cheek.

"Ain't used to keepin' store," the tall man commented, "but it sure gives a man a chance to set. The Navajos have mostly gone back inside to the high country with their sheep. I ain't seen an Indian in two weeks."

The stocky man tamped his pipe with a middle finger, and looked out the window. He always sat where he could see outside, for it kept him from the cramped feeling he got from being bottled up too tight. He was unused to buildings except in their ruined state.

"You goin' back in, Gay?" The lanky man was glad of company, for he was the gregarious sort who liked to talk even when he had little to talk about.

"Uh-huh." Gay Cooley was watching the two riders he could see through the window. They had come from the north, but were now approaching from the west; obviously they had wanted to see what horses might be at the hitch rail before they came on in. One of the riders was a woman, riding side-saddle. A woman in this country was an uncommon sight.

After a few minutes, Gay Cooley struck a match. When he had inhaled deeply, then exhaled, he commented, "Visitors, Skin. Better dust off your manners. There's a lady."

Startled, the tall man slid from the counter to stare out the window. "Well, I d'clare! A real, live lady"

The riders walked their horses to the rail and the man dismounted, offering some low-voiced comment to the woman, who remained in the saddle.

"Skittish," Gay commented.

"What's that? What did you say?"

"Nothing. Talking to myself. Just pay me no mind."

Matt Keelock pushed the door wide with the barrel of his Winchester, then stepped in. The movement allowed him to have the muzzle of the gun pointed into the store, at hip level, without it seeming in any way discourteous to those within.

Gay Cooley's eyes glinted at the gesture and he started to speak, then closed his lips on his pipe. Matt

Keelock had looked at him as though he were a stranger.

"Place around here for a lady to freshen up? My wife's ridden a far piece."

"Sure as shootin'." Skin gestured toward a door behind the counter. "Boss lives back there, and he's got it fixed for his own woman. You go right to it."

Matt spoke over his shoulder, then walked on in. To have helped Kris down would mean to turn his back on the store and the men within, and that he was not prepared to do. He was not worried much about Gay Cooley, although he had not seen him for several years.

"We'll need supplies." Matt placed a carefully written list on the counter. "Nearest place west will be Prescott, won't it?"

"Uh-huh." Skin glanced at the door, then his eyes went wide as he saw Kris. Her beauty brought a change to the plain room.

"Goin' to Californy?" he asked.

"No ... somewhere around Prescott. Maybe Skull Valley."

Kris went through the door behind the counter, and Skin started moving around, picking up items. Matt Keelock walked over the the the stove.

"How's the trail west of here?" he asked Cooley.

The older man glanced up, mildly amused. "Good enough ... I've been that way a time or two."

Under his breath Gay said, "You the one shot that man down to Freedom?"

"Yes."

"Description sounded like you. The shootin' didn't."

"He was facing the bar, half-turned and drew. My first shot got him back of the left shoulder, the second in the spine. He'd been standing left side toward the door, and he drew from his waistband and fired from under his left arm. It was a fair shooting."

"Never doubted it."

Skin was busy piling up packages, measuring.

"They've hired themselves a marshal. Stranger ... a big, cold-faced man."

"Neerland?"

Cooley glanced up sharply. "You know him?"

"We had words." Matt gestured toward the back room. "Over her."

There was a moment of silence, during which Skin continued his ambling about the store, searching for the various things. Unfamiliar as he was with the stock—for he had been asked to care for it only while the trader was over in Prescott on business—he was slow, but Matt was in no hurry, now that he had found Cooley.

"Three men back there," he said. "Do you know them?"

Gay Cooley hesitated, then replied, "No ... don't think I do. One of them might be Neerland, as you call him."

"There will be others. I led that posse to Mormon Well."

"Heard so." Cooley lowered his feet to the floor. "Do 'em no good. I've known where it was for years, and it never did me any good." He glanced up at Matt Keelock. "You huntin' the Lost Wagons yourself?"

"Me? Hell, no! Only kind of gold I want is on four hoofs ... a stallion."

"Seen him a time or two," Cooley said. "That's a lot of horse, man."

"Anybody should ask you, I'm riding out for Prescott and Skull Valley. I'm going to locate over there."

"Good country."

Gay Cooley was not a man either to comment or to ask questions, but he was well aware that Keelock would not be going to Prescott. Keelock was about horses the way he was about that Lost Wagon treasure.

Kris came back into the room, and Cooley stared. God! he thought. What a woman!

Matt Keelock picked up his sacked supplies and

carried them outside to his pack animals. As he packed up, he watched the trail. He would be uneasy until he got clear away and into the hills again.

Gay Cooley and Skin went to the door, watching him.

As he drew the last hitch tight, Kris came from the door and he helped her into the saddle.

"You get over around Skull Valley," he said, "you boys look me up. You'll be most welcome."

"Somebody comin'," Cooley remarked. "Two riders."

Kris spoke urgently. "Matt!"

"It's all right." They were only a couple of hundred yards off, coming in from the west, which could mean the south and, possibly, Freedom. They were riding easily, and seemed unworried about anything. Almost without movement, Matt shifted his position just enough to keep Kris out of the line of fire.

The men were coming on, trotting their horses now as they drew near. Keelock made a show of tightening the cinch on his horse, keeping the animal between himself and them.

They rode up, glancing sharply at him. He knew them both, for he had seen them from the dry wash ... they were from the posse that had trailed him after the shooting in Freedom.

Short turned his horse to the hitch rail and got down. He looked toward the door and saw Gay Cooley step aside. Something in Cooley's manner made Short turn his head sharp around. And in that instant, his instinct warned him—this was the man.

He stood flat-footed, feet slightly apart, looking over his shoulder. It was an awkward position from which to start a draw, for he must turn completely around in order to bring his gun to bear on the target. And he could not see McAlpin, who was behind him and to his left.

Keelock's shift of position had both men under his

gun. McAlpin, all unaware, had stopped to loosen his cinch, and Short was sweating.

"That's what I like," he said abruptly. "A man who's so damn' careful of his horse!"

"Now what's eatin' you?" McAlpin's tone showed his astonishment. "I—"

Then his eyes registered on Matt Keelock and he was still, for the readiness in the man was obvious.

"You boys better unbuckle," Keelock suggested mildly. "This here's a mighty peaceful place, and we'd hate to get it all over with blood. You boys just let those belts fall."

He was holding the Winchester, and the range was perfect. At that distance, there was no chance at all of his missing, and they both knew it.

"Now, see here!" McAlpin began. "I—"

"Shut up," Short said, "and drop your belt!"

Both gun belts fell, and then Keelock gestured to Skin. "You there, storekeeper, move in and snake those guns away from there, and don't get lined up between us. I might mistake your intentions."

When the gun belts were out of the way, Keelock came out from behind his horse. "Now you boys back up and sit down. I'm going to read you from the Book."

Briefly, concisely, he told them of the gun battle forced on him by Johnny Webb; and when he had finished, he added, "I don't blame you boys for hunting me the first time because you didn't know no better. Now you do."

"What's that mean?" Short demanded belligerently.

"It means that if I ever catch you on my trail again I'm going to take it as unfriendly."

"We ain't huntin' you," McAlpin protested. "We figured to have a look for the Lost Wagons."

"That's your privilege. Only keep this in mind: If I catch you on my back trail, no matter what you're hunting, I'll stake each of you to six feet of northern Arizona that nobody will ever take away from you."

Deliberately, he turned his back and walked to his horse. He stepped into the saddle, then turned his horse. Neither man had moved.

But it was not in Short to keep still. "We don't give a damn what you do. If Bill Chesney doesn't get you, Neerland will."

Matt Keelock ignored the remark and started off, following Kris. He glanced back once. Neither man moved from his seat until they were crossing the low hill, and then there was no hurry in them.

"They were afraid of you," Kristina said.

"No, Kris, they weren't afraid. Only I had them dead to rights, and only a damned fool would gamble at such a time. Under other conditions, and if they wanted me bad enough, they'd not hesitate."

"That took nerve."

"A man does what he has to."

They rode steadily westward. Keelock studied his back trail from time to time, but there was no dust, no indication that they might be followed.

"You knew that man back there."

"Gay Cooley? Yes, I've known him for quite a while. If anybody ever finds the Lost Wagons, it will be him."

"Nobody can be sure about a thing like that. It could be anybody. It could be found by accident." Then her mood changed. She looked back quickly, suddenly worried. "Matt, did they believe us? Will they believe we left the country?"

"We'll hope so. We'll just have to hope so. And in the meanwhile, we're going back after those horses."

"But if you get the horses, won't you go to Prescott? Won't they find you then?"

"Maybe. I'm figuring they'll look there, they won't find us, and they'll give up on that part of the country."

He glanced toward their shadows, estimating the time. There was a stretch of blown sand ahead, and he wanted to reach it at nightfall; for that sand would hold no tracks that could be identified, and if it was dark enough there would be no eye to see when they turned off.

In the west the sky was ablaze with the sunset glow. Over there lay the Painted Desert and the Canyon of the Colorado, north lay Echo Cliffs, where the trail lay. But they would not take that known trail; theirs would be an ancient Indian trail, old before time began, a trail that led northward toward the Crossing of the Fathers, but a trail no longer used.

Such trails he had always known, and such were the trails he loved the best.

nine

From the rim near War God Spring, Matt Keelock studied the vast broken land to the south. Using the field glasses, he ignored no patch of shadow, no fold or crack in the land. In the ten days since leaving the trade store at Tuba City they had seen no evidence of pursuit, nor had they seen the tracks of the golden stallion.

Obviously, something had frightened the mustangs from their accustomed haunts, but where had they gone? That they occasionally came here to War God Spring, Matt knew. There was lush grass, plenty of good water, and there was the shade of aspens and tall pines.

All morning he had had the feeling of being watched, the sense of something happening of which he was unaware, but he had seen neither smoke nor dust, nothing to give a reason for his worry. At last he lowered the glasses and went back to camp.

Behind him, and many miles off across the country

he had been studying, a small puff of dust appeared, faded, then grew and maintained a course toward the northeast.

At the fire, Kris looked up. "Matt, I've been thinking. Let's ride back to Organ Rock where we saw them last."

"Why there?"

"That stallion was going somewhere, Matt. I think he was taking his herd to some particular place, but when they saw us they veered off. If we go back we might find some tracks."

It was good thinking, and he told her so. Animals were notional, and if they took a notion to go somewhere, they would usually keep trying until they made it.

The trouble was, he knew of no direct route, although there might well be one. He disliked going back toward the south and the proximity of any searchers, while to the north the country was crossed by the San Juan River and its deep, winding canyon. War God Spring was good water, and it was the perfect hideaway. Getting out of it toward the south would take him right into the trail through Marsh Pass, the last place he wanted to be.

He had come to War God Spring half expecting to find the stallion there, but the only tracks were old ones. Only the Navajos knew the place—unless perhaps, Gay Cooley knew of it ... but every hour increased their danger.

The coffee tasted good. He nursed a cup in his hands and looked across the fire at Kris. "How about it? Have you had enough of this? I mean a girl like you ... used to so much."

She smiled. "Matt, I left nothing behind me that mattered. Oh, I will admit that once in a while I think of what all my friends may be doing, but I've no desire to be back there again. Father said I was a throwback to the Vikings, that there was wildness in me."

She looked around, then her eyes went back to Matt. "You must believe this. I am happier than I have ever been before."

Before daylight the next morning they abandoned the spring, taking a faint Indian trail across Rainbow Plateau. They descended to Piute Creek by a switchback trail.

Matt was worried, and said as much. "I don't know this part of the country, Kris. Unless we can find a way to get down off Piute Mesa, we may have to turn south."

When a man had a woman riding with him he asked for trouble, for his attention was distracted in planning for her, thinking of her welfare. For himself, it mattered little. He was accustomed to hardship, accustomed to thirst, hunger, heat, cold, and trails that made the hair crawl on the back of his neck. Now he must hesitate ... not that Kris would be willing to receive privileged treatment if she became aware of it.

There was a trace of water in the bottom of Nakia Wash, left over from a recent rain. He allowed the horses a breather, for the trail was hard, and might be harder. At this point there was a trail coming in from the south, a well-marked trail, which must be one he had heard of that led to ruins farther along the mesa.

Leaving the water, he walked the horses for a short distance, then returned and brushed out their tracks and sifted dust over the brushing.

Another trail, a dim one, completely vanished in places, led them to the rim of the cliff. Below them lay the gap toward which the wild bunch had been pointing. Across Nakia Canyon to the north was No Man's Mesa, lifting its ominous bulk against the sky.

Here again they waited while he studied the land below them. There must be a place below to rest. They had come at least thirty miles that day, and the animals were tired.

Directly across the canyon, and perhaps a thousand

feet lower, was the top of Nakia Mesa. Beyond the canyon there appeared to be a cove among the trees, which looked to be a secure place. And there they would be within a short distance of the trail the wild horses had followed.

Usually such bands of wild horses follow a route they establish over a wide sweep of country, a route that may make a circle of forty or fifty miles, but that constantly returns to grass and water.

The stars were out when they reached the cove. When Matt reached up to help Kris from the saddle she almost fell into his arms.

"I am sorry," he said, and he held her in his arms for a moment. "Truly sorry."

"For better or worse, Matt ... remember? I asked for this. I bought it with my eyes wide open." She drew back her head to look at him. "But I *am* tired!"

He left her with the horses and went off into the night, but he was back almost at once. He led them through the brush and up a steep trail to a small bench among the rocks and trees above the cove.

With a fire going in a corner of the rocks, under a shelving ledge, Kris prepared a meal. While she worked by the fire, Matt cleaned and oiled his Winchester, then his six-gun. Then he went to his pack for his spare Colt, and cleaned it.

When they sat down to eat, Kris said, "Do you think they'll find us, Matt?"

"They will."

"What will we do?"

"When the waiting is over, we will do what we can."

Shortly before dawn he woke suddenly, and his eyes went at once to the horses. They were standing, heads up, listening.

At first he heard nothing; then came a rustle of faroff movement. The sound grew louder and he heard horses, many horses, passing in the night.

At daybreak, while Kris prepared breakfast, he

went to the canyon and found tracks—thirty or forty
unshod horses, among them the tracks of the golden
stallion. They seemed to have gone north, up Nakia
Canyon.

They ate swiftly, then saddled up and rode out on
the trail of the wild bunch.

Bill Chesney was irritable. He glared at Neill.
"Sometimes I think you don't care whether we find
that Key-Lock man or not."

The hard riding of the past few weeks had put an
edge to Neill's temper too, and he was growing up.
Too long he had worried about what Bill Chesney
thought, and a man earned respect not by following
in another man's tracks, but by making his own.

"I am not riding to kill a man. If he shot Johnny in
the back he deserves hanging, but he should get a
chance to tell his side of it. He claims it was a fair
shooting."

"*Claims?*" Chesney's tone was ugly. "What did you
expect him to do—*confess?*"

"He had his chance if he wanted to kill. He could
have had one or more of us and gotten off down that
wash. And when it comes to that, Bill, you know as
well as I do that Johnny was a trouble-hunter. He
fancied himself with those guns of his."

"You tryin' to tell *me* about *Johnny?* Why, you—"

"Take it easy, Bill." Kimmel spoke with quiet authority. "You've got no call to ride Neill."

Chesney wheeled on Kimmel. "You, too?"

Neill might be an uncertain quantity, but Kimmel
was not. Whatever else he might be, Kimmel was
definitely a dangerous man to tangle with in any kind
of a fight. Now, through the heat of Chesney's anger
blew the cool wind of sanity. Kimmel, relaxed, rested
on one elbow, saying nothing more.

The fire crackled in the night's stillness, and Neill
added fuel to it. Then he commented, "I came along
because I intend to see fair play. We don't know the

circumstances of the killing and we don't know this man. If you ask me, he shapes up like somebody to ride the river with, as Sam would say. It might just be that Johnny tackled too much man."

"Hell, nobody was as fast as Johnny," Chesney declared but with less heat.

"Nobody? Not even Jim Courtright, or Clay Allison? Or Wild Bill?"

"That Key-Lock man is no Wild Bill."

"You can't be sure, Bill. If you can read anything at all from a man's trail, this one is a curly wolf."

In the silence that followed this remark, the leaves were restless, and the flames leaned before a puff of wind.

"Before this here is over," Kimmel said, "somebody is sure going to buy chips to make him show his hand."

"Look at it this way, Bill," Neill said quietly. "We're starting a new town. Sure, it isn't much of a place yet, but it can be. You and me, we'll raise our families there, and we don't want it to start off with the lynching of an innocent man."

Chesney made no reply, but his jaw was set hard and his face seemed closed to reason.

Neill got up to gather more fuel, but he paused for several minutes, hands on hips, and looked up at the stars. Well, he had asserted himself, at least. He had said what he had to say, and he felt better because of it. He wanted friends, of course, but the friends a man had must accept him on his own terms, and not because he merely stepped in their tracks.

Half the trouble in the world, he thought, was probably caused because right-thinking people kept their mouths shut instead of speaking up and saying what they believed.

Nobody knew what had happened in that saloon except Johnny and the man they hunted. All agreed that the Key-Lock man had to go get his gun from his pack, and that did not argue that he was a trouble-

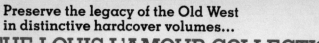

Preserve the legacy of the Old West in distinctive hardcover volumes...

THE LOUIS L'AMOUR COLLECTION

Now you and your family can experience the authentic Old West...its rich lore and legend in a rugged, handsome series: The Louis L'Amour Collection—superb hardcover Heritage Editions, meticulously bound in padded Sierra-brown leatherette.

Each matching volume— with the look and feel of hand-rubbed saddle leather—is an enduring testament to our unique American past...a tribute to the narrative power of Louis L'Amour, the most popular writer of frontier adventures who ever lived.

Start your Louis L'Amour Collection now with FLINT—a gripping novel of murder and revenge—FREE for 10 days. If you decide to keep it, further volumes may be previewed each month, also for 10 days free. Each volume contributes to an impressive home library, certain to become a treasured family heirloom...to be enjoyed again and again.

Mail the card at right today.

Now in handsome Heritage Editions

Each matching 6" x 9" volume in The Collection is bound in rich Sierra-brown leatherette, with padded covers and embossed gold title... creating an enduring family library of distinction.

hunter. It could be that Johnny had tried to run up a score against the wrong man.

Some men would naturally back down. Neill himself had kept his mouth shut more than once in the past few years. He was a stranger and he did not know the people or the country, and it was good to wait until you knew what you were talking about. But Kimmel had stood his ground against Chesney, and you could bet that the next time Chesney rode out he would want Kimmel with him. He had sand, and they all knew it.

Neill was some distance from the fire when he heard Chesney grumbling. ". . . too big for his britches."

"You lay off him," Kimmel was saying. "That boy's solid. You push him and you're goin' to have to shoot him or get shot."

"Him?"

The incredulity in Chesney's voice made Neill flush with anger and shame.

"Don't be a damn' fool, Bill. He was new to the country, so he's walked soft and listened. Well, he's eaten the dust and tasted the salt, and from here on he'll make his own tracks."

When they bedded down for the night, they were just eleven miles from Neerland and his two men; and the two fires formed the base corners of a triangle at the point of which were Kris and Matt Keelock.

The desert wind that stirred the smoke of their two fires moved north and, channeled by the canyons, stirred the smoke of the Keelock fire also. And only a little farther north, that smoke was smelled by a golden stallion that tossed his head irritably, staring uneasily into the wind.

Matt Keelock woke from a heavy sleep with the lemon light of day showing faint across the eastern sky. The snort of a horse had awakened him and his eyes went, as always, toward his buckskin, whose ways he knew well. The animal had his head up, nostrils distended, and was staring toward the mouth of the cove.

"Quiet, boy! Quiet now!" Rifle in hand, Matt moved to the trees at the edge of the bench. Moments passed, and he saw nothing, heard no sound.

His boots were back at camp, and his shirt. He hesitated, wanting to go back and get dressed. A man caught without boots in this country was in trouble. He was about to turn away when some suggestion of movement arrested his attention. It was no more than a shift in a shadow—an outline that had not seemed to be there before . . . or was he imagining things?

Suddenly Kris was beside him, carrying his boots, his shirt and gun belt. "Watch that," he said, indicating the place, and he handed her the rifle. Then he sat down swiftly and tugged on his boots. When he stood up she gave back his rifle.

"Nothing," she said.

But there had been something down there. He stared, looked away, then looked past the spot to put it in the outer limits of his gaze. Yes, there was something or somebody down there. He put down his rifle and calmly got into his shirt.

All right . . . so they were here. He had done what he could to avoid trouble, so if they came to him now they had to put their bullets on the line. From here on out, it was pay to play.

Then suddenly a man appeared in sight, and he was both young and a complete stranger.

He wore a battered hat, a cowhide vest, and a pair of tied-down guns. He carried a Henry rifle in his hands, and he seemed to be looking for something— some landmark, some object.

They stood silent, watching as the man came nearer to where they stood. He looked at the mesa opposite, then turned and looked up, straight toward them. They were back under the trees, fronted by brush, and there was scarcely a chance that they could be seen—and in fact the man did not see them.

"He isn't hunting tracks," Matt whispered, "so whatever he's looking for, it isn't us."

"What else would he be hunting?"

The Lost Wagons ...

But surely not way up here! The Lost Wagons were south of here a good many miles ... ten or fifteen, anyway. Or were they? Something in the stranger's manner implied knowledge, for he was not looking about at random. He was searching for some definite thing, or some particular place.

If he was looking for the Lost Wagons he should have been searching for wheels, or for some remnant of the wagons themselves, for the bolts or the hubs of the wheels, which were of hardwood and virtually indestructible in this desert country. But it seemed obvious that he was looking for some landmark, some sign on the mountains themselves.

And then Matt heard another sound, the faintest whisper of rough material against rock. It came from behind him. He turned swiftly, dropping to one knee, Winchester lifted for firing.

A man stood just inside the rim of brush, hands lifted. It was Gay Cooley.

Matt remained where he was, the rifle held steady. Gay came toward them, keeping his hands high. Behind him walked his horse, followed by a pack horse. When he was within twenty yards, Matt stopped him.

"Lost something?"

Gay grinned. "The Lost Wagons. You know me."

"I don't take kindly to folks who come up behind me."

"Don't blame you. But you'd better take to me, because I may be the only friend you've got."

"So?"

"After you left, Bill Chesney showed up. Neill and Kimmel were with him. Short and McAlpin told them about you two, but Chesney wouldn't buy the Skull Valley story."

"We tried."

"Neerland is already up here with two other men."

Matt gestured toward the man below them. "That one of them?"

Gay Cooley stepped nearer, then leaned forward and peered. He swore softly. "Matt, that's Muley. That's the kid who was with the gold wagons."

Lost to his surroundings, Muley moved along the foot of the mesa near them. "Look at him!" Cooley whispered hoarsely. "He knows where he is! He's found something!"

It did look that way, for Muley was moving along more rapidly, his excitement obvious. If he had not found a sign or landmark, he certainly believed he had.

At that moment there was a rattle of hoofs and a shout. "*Muley!* Damn it, man! Where you going?"

The rider was a stocky, barrel-chested stranger, who must be the other man with Neerland.

"You better high-tail it back. He's sore as a galled mule, you traipsing off like that. What you huntin'?"

"Scoutin' tracks. Thought I seen something."

"All right, let's go back."

The newcomer turned his mount and for an instant his back was full on Muley. The Winchester lifted slowly, then halted.

Gay Cooley glanced over at Matt. "That gent will never come closer and not get killed," he said. "Ol' Muley was ready. You could see it in every line of him."

"That could be the man—The one who killed all those men," Matt said.

"*Muley?*" Gay Cooley's tone was not as incredulous as it might have been. Evidently the thought had occurred to him too. "He was only a youngster."

"How old do you have to be?" Keelock inquired dryly. "I was fightin' Indians when I was twelve."

The two riders turned and rode away, and Gay Cooley slowly relaxed. Matt could see the beads of sweat on his forehead.

"You see what that means? Everybody's been wrong. Everybody believed it was south of here, and everybody has looked to the south. You can just bet Muley saw something he recognized, and whatever it was told him he was close to the Lost Wagons."

He looked at Kris, then back at Matt Keelock. "I'm goin' to be a rich man, you see that, don't you?"

"I see you aren't alone. Those boys out there are huntin' me, but if they get the smell of gold they'll forget all about me. You find that gold now, Gay, and you're chewin' on grief."

Gay Cooley was not listening. "Matt, look at it this way. That Muley boy, they left him tied when they went off to hide that gold. So what could he recognize? Either the place where he was tied up, or something he saw before or after." Cooley looked around, dazed with the shock of it. "Matt, I'd make a fancy bet that gold ain't a mile from us right this minute . . . and maybe closer!"

Matt was looking in the direction in which the two men had disappeared. If Muley was truly the boy who had been with the wagons, he would not want to leave the area, now that he was so close to the treasure. So what would he do? Would he lose himself and let them go on without him? Would he resort to murder again, as he seemed to have done before? In any case, Matt Keelock knew that the noose was slowly tightening about his own neck.

There was no place to go from here. To the north lay the canyon of the San Juan, only a few miles away. Towering cliffs were all about, and all travel was channeled by them. To the east lay the valley of the weird monuments, but miles of open country were all around them.

With a woman to think of, there was only one thing

to do—stay where he was, make no tracks, and hope they would pass him by.

"I'm goin' down there," Gay Cooley said, and he was on his feet, rifle in hand.

But before he could take a step, Matt spoke up. "I can't let you go, Cooley. You've got to stay with us."

In his hand, Matt Keelock held a six-shooter.

ten

Shocked, Kris stared at her husband. Gay Cooley, his Winchester in his hand, measured the chances and did not like them. He would have to swing that gun up and grasp the trigger, cock and fire. No, he did not like the chances at all.

"What is this, Matt? You and me ... I figured we were friends."

"We are. You never had a friend better than me, Cooley, but you've the gold fever on you. If you go down there now they'll see you, or they'll find your sign, and they'll come hunting. When they do, they'll find Kris and me. I can't let you go down there, Gay."

Cooley relaxed. "Hell, man! You had me scared. I figured maybe you wanted that gold for yourself." His eyes probed Matt's. "You sure that ain't in your mind?"

"I'm after horses."

"All right, put that gun away. I'll stand by until

they pull out, or until one of them finds that gold. If they do, all bets are off."

"Why, that's right enough, Cooley. You've hunted that gold long enough to lay claim to it, as far as I'm concerned. If it comes to that, you can go down there shootin', and Kris and me will take our chances. Only let's not buy anything until it's offered us."

Gay Cooley sat down in the shade of a tree and placed his rifle beside him, butt on the ground. He was too experienced a man to leave room for misunderstanding.

He looked at Keelock. "Matt, you surely forked that gun out of somewhere mighty fast. I didn't know you could handle a Colt like that."

Keelock shrugged. "Gay, a man has it, or he hasn't. I mean, you can practice, you can better yourself, but if a man has the right coordination ... well, it's a come-natural thing, I say."

"You could put notches on that gun."

"That's a tin-horn's trick, an' well you know it."

Kris sat down, her legs trembling. She had been shocked and frightened. Now, despite the swift clearing of the air, she knew trouble was coming, and both men knew it also. Would there be trouble from Cooley? Would he resent what had happened?

They waited while the hours went by. Bees buzzed under the trees ... it seemed almost peaceful. From time to time the horses stamped, switched their tails at flies, or snorted a little. Nobody spoke, and the morning worked its way into afternoon.

"Do you think they have gone, Matt?" Kris asked.

"No."

"That Muley ain't gone—not far, anyway." Cooley spoke with assurance. "Not with all that gold waiting."

He leaned back, put his hands behind his head, and stared at the cliffs. Now, where could that gold be? Supposing there was little time, and that gold had to be taken where horses could go, and buried or hidden. Wild as the country was, and broken up as it was, there were only a few directions in which a man could travel.

Now, if he knew how long they had been gone ... Muley surely knew that. They would scarcely have gone to the towering cliff opposite, the cliff of Piute Mesa. No, the gold must be behind them, or to the north or south. And he favored the Nakia Mesa, right behind them.

Despite himself, studying the country for signs of movement, Matt Keelock was thinking in the same way. He was also thinking about Gay Cooley.

Somewhere out there were Neerland, Muley, and that other rider. Somewhere out there, too, were Bill Chesney and those with him ... there'd be five in that lot now, with Short and McAlpin joined up.

Nobody spoke of food, though all of them were hungry. The smoke of a fire might bring down the very trouble they sought to avoid.

Gay Cooley had recognized Muley. The thought came suddenly to Matt, and he scowled. Cooley noticed the scowl and glanced away, but Matt turned the idea over in his mind. How could Cooley have known Muley?

He must have been one of the original group, or he had seen Muley in Santa Fe.

And Matt Keelock, with enemies all about, realized that here in his own camp there might be another. Whatever happened, he must not forget about Gay Cooley.

"Matt. ... ?"

He turned and followed Kris's pointing finger. The horses were there, the wild bunch led by the golden stallion.

"Look, Gay." All else was forgotten. "You can have your gold. That's what I want."

The wild bunch were moving along a sunlit trail not fifty yards away. The wind was from them and toward the watchers, and the horses showed no awareness of the presence of men as they moved slowly but steadily along the valley floor. The stallion was magnificent, but scarcely more so than several of the mares.

"By the Lord Harry," Gay Cooley exclaimed reverently, "I don't blame you!"

Suddenly tense, he went on, "That there mare ... the one with the three white stockings and the scar on the shoulder ... now that one's no youngster."

Matt Keelock shrugged. "She's old, no doubt about it, but there's plenty of young stuff in that bunch."

He was oblivious to everything but the horses; but Kris, watching Cooley, was struck by the man's sudden interest. Cooley was not looking at the stallion at all, but at the old, scarred mare that followed him.

"We'll wait," Matt said, "and let them get a lead on us. I want to trail along and see where they go."

Bill Chesney, riding north, drew rein when he saw the Indians. There were five of them, including a squaw and two children. Of the two men, the younger was known to Chesney as Cheap Jim from his habit of offering his services "cheap." He was a first-class rider, and had often worked for Chesney. A hard man in so many ways, Chesney demanded hard work from anyone employed by him. On the other hand, his table provided the best food in the country, and his chuck wagon never lacked for extras.

"Jim, you want a trackin' job?" Chesney asked now.

The Navajo shook his head. "I ride to Tuba City." His black eyes went from one to another, then back to Chesney. "You hunt?"

"A white man ... might be a woman with him."

Jim hesitated. It was never the Indian way to offer information. On the other hand, this man was his friend, and not many white ranchers were eager to employ an Indian rider.

"Back there," he gestured toward Piute Mesa, "I see trail ... five, six horses, two riders."

He explained they had been camped at the old ruin, and when starting south had seen the dust, and later had found no trail. Curious, they had scouted around, picking up the trail farther along and following it until it went down the cliff into the canyon.

When the Navajos had gone on, Chesney expressed his triumph. "There it is, boys! We've got 'em now!"

Neill looked at him, and started to speak, but hesitated. There was no need to make an issue of it now. Wait until they had met the Key-Lock man and faced him. A man could buy trouble by trying to cross bridges before reaching them, and many an issue disappeared before it actually became a matter of trouble.

What he had started to ask was whether Chesney planned to hang the Key-Lock man right in front of his wife. He had desisted, but now the feeling of doom was on him again. He looked around uneasily. So far, the Key-Lock man had not chosen to make a fight of it, but there was a limit to any man's patience.

From the rim of the cliff, they saw far below them a moving dust cloud. Not large, but enough to indicate several horses.

"What do you make of it, Neill?" Chesney asked.

"Wild horses." Neill had the best eyesight of the lot. "Quite a bunch of them, and they are taking it easy."

Bill Chesney's common sense told him it was unlikely that a pursued man would ride further north. The San Juan River cut across the country and, so far as Chesney knew, there was no crossing for many miles. No Man's Mesa split the country in half, but the man they sought should be right down there somewhere. He could not be far.

He was just about to give the word to start down the trail when he saw them.

Three riders and several pack animals. They came down off what appeared to be a bench and started

north, following the wild horses, intentionally or by
accident.

"We've got 'em, boys!" Chesney fought back his
excitement. "There they go!"

"There's three of them," Neill objected. "If that's
the Key-Lock man and his wife, then who is the other
one?"

Nobody answered. Chesney had turned his horse
down the trail. *Now, by the Lord! Now!* he was
saying it over and over as he went down the trail.

Short, remembering Keelock at Tuba City, felt a
coldness inside him, and a tightness at the back of his
neck. Keelock had told them what he would do if he
found them on his trail again, and here they were,
with him down there.

"I've got to kill him. Short said the words softly to
himself. *I've got to get him before he gets me. To hell
with hanging! I'm goin' to shoot.*

He dropped back alongside McAlpin. "He meant
what he said, Mac. That Key-Lock man surely meant
what he said."

"What'll we do?"

"Kill him . . . shoot first and quick."

"Bill wants to hang him. He's set on usin' that rope."

"The hell with him!"

"What'll we do? What can we do?"

"He's got a woman with him. He'll want to talk, to
get her out of it. Well, we'll let Chesney talk. We'll
shoot."

"Wonder where that Neerland is," McAlpin said.

Short had forgotten him, but it did not seem to
matter now. "He's out of it now. This is Keelock and
us."

The five men went down the switch-back trail in
the prime of the morning. The sun was upon them,
warm and pleasant after the night's chill. Neill rode
third, right behind Kimmel, and he knew he was in
trouble. It was all well and good to make a stand, to
speak your piece and have it listened to; but now,

perhaps within a few minutes, certainly within a few hours, he would have to make his stand in the face of armed men. And past friendships would not count now. With Chesney feeling the way he did, it might become a matter of shooting between them, and he shrank from that. And that was where his weakness lay, the weakness of a man who wants to stand for what is right and just. For Neill would hesitate to kill, while the fanatics never hesitated.

But there were just men who had not hesitated. Who was that vigilante up Montana way? Beidler ... he had killed, and rightly so, for there had been no other way. Yet had he ever been asked to shoot down a friend, or a man he respected?

Neill glanced at Kimmel. Where would he stand? He was a tough man, a veteran of several shooting scrapes, and as many Indian fights. If anyone among them could restrain Chesney it would be Kimmel, for he had done it before. He would not hesitate to kill, but he did not seem to possess the hatred that Chesney did.

A stone fell away and rattled long among the rocks below. They turned another bend of the switch-back and faced the way the three riders had traveled, but they were no longer visible.

The low-voiced talk between McAlpin and Short had ceased. Neill felt his mouth becoming dry, as it always did in tense moments. How far away were they, he wondered.

One more switch-back and they touched bottom. Bill Chesney touched a spur to his horse and in a long lope he led off, riding northward, up the valley. On their left were the sheer cliffs of Piute Mesa; on their right, Nakia Canyon, and beyond it the ominous black bulk of No Man's Mesa.

"We've got him!" Chesney was hot with eagerness. "We've got him now!"

Neill closed in beside Kimmel. "These cliffs run to the river?"

"Almost." Kimmel spoke loudly, over the sound of rushing hoofs. "Piute swings away to the west and closes in on the river. It's a death trap thataway."

"How about No Man's Mesa?"

Kimmel pointed with the barrel of his Winchester. "She heads up about a mile this side of the river. There's a trail around the end into Copper Canyon!"

Chesney turned in his saddle. "Damn it, why can't you shut up? He'll hear that yelling all the way to the San Juan!"

The level ground ended, narrowing down a good bit, and they slowed their horses to a walk and rode single file. The sun had grown hot and the dark shadows below the western wall of No Man's called to them of coolness, but their eyes were ahead, restless with the nearing danger.

Between the towering walls where they rode was a space of nearly three miles, but talus slopes at the base of the walls narrowed it down, and the cut made by Nakia Canyon narrowed the area which they must search.

Neill felt the sweat trickling down his chest under his shirt. He wished again that Hardin was here, Hardin with his cool head and his sense of balance, his quiet words that always seemed to take the sharp edge off things. Neill was riding alone, and he knew it. No one in this lot was surely on his side, for Kimmel was only a doubtful chance. Nobody ever knew what he thought or believed.

They were riding to kill a man, and with each step they drew nearer to their aim ... to kill a man who might be innocent, a newly wed man who rode with his bride.

And who was the third party with them, and where did he stand?

Matt Keelock drew rein. The wild horses were close ahead now. He had first to see where they were going, for he had no wish to stampede them over the cliffs into the San Juan. He had never touched the river at this point, but for most of its miles it lay between towering walls.

He felt jumpy inside, but not because of the horses. He turned in his saddle and looked back.

Nothing. . . .

He glanced at his wife. "You all right, Kris?"

She nodded, but behind the stillness of her face he read worry, for he was coming to know her moods now. A branch canyon opened on their right, and suddenly, without a second's hesitation, he turned into it. The others followed.

"Now, what was that for?" Cooley asked. "I thought you wanted those horses?"

"I've got a hunch."

Kris merely looked at him, but Cooley grumbled, "You were right on those horses, Matt. Why leave them now?"

Keelock ignored him. He was looking around quickly for an escape. His sudden move might have run them into a box canyon, one from which there was no way out. The canyon seemed to head up on No Man's itself. He rode slowly, and when the wall on the south became low at one spot, he drew up. "Wait here," he said and, turning the buckskin, he went back down the canyon.

There were few tracks, and little enough he could do about them except in a place or two. He did what he could to obliterate their trail, then rode back and led the way up the wall.

"You ain't much better off," Cooley said. "Now you've got that canyon behind you, and there's another one south. Only way you can get out of here that I know of is back across Nakia."

Where they had stopped there was desert growth and slabs of broken rock, but no good shelter. They were on rising ground where the country sloped steeply back to the abrupt cliffs of No Man's Mesa.

And then he saw them, and almost at the same

moment the man riding the lead horse turned his head and glanced up the mountain. He reined in so sharply that his horse reared, and as one man the others turned their heads and looked up toward Keelock.

Kris . . . I've got to save Kris.

"Stay here," he ordered brusquely. Then he turned his buckskin and rode down the wall to meet them.

eleven

So Matt Keelock rode to the combat through a sunlit morning, sitting lazy in the saddle, right hand resting on his thigh. He rode down with his mind empty, his ears hearing only the hoof falls of his horse and the creak of his saddle leather.

The buckskin knew. Matt could sense it in every movement of the horse. The buckskin knew, just as a good cutting horse knows what is about to happen as it approaches a herd of cattle. The buckskin was a good cutting horse, but he was more. He was a horse with a genuine zest for combat.

Matt Keelock had not wanted a fight, but they were bringing it to him, and if the shooting had begun with Kris beside him she might have been killed. So he rode to meet them, giving no more thought to Gay Cooley. He expected no help from him, because this was not Cooley's fight ... it was his, and his alone.

The distance was narrowing down. He looked at no

man in particular, his eyes holding them all, to register each movement. Two of the riders held back and to one side. Now what did that mean? Were they drawing out of it? Were they getting out before shooting started? Or did they plan a flanking movement?

When no more than a hundred yards off, he drew up suddenly. On his left were several low, gnarled cedars that grew up from a ledge of rock perhaps three feet high. On his right was a cleft in the rock that dropped away steeply into the canyon that cut down from No Man's Mesa.

Loosening his boots in the stirrups, he held himself still and ready, and moved forward a little farther.

At fifty yards he suddenly called out, "All right, hold up there!"

They stopped, and he said, "I told you that was a fair shooting. Your trouble-hunting friend jumped me unarmed, told me to heel myself and come back, and when I started in the door he drew and shot across his body and under his arm at me. I returned his fire, and the shots took him in the side and back."

"Like hell!" Chesney shouted. "You murdered him, and you'll hang!" He came on a few steps, then drew up again. "You never saw the day you could beat Johnny with a gun!"

"How about it, *amigo?*" Matt Keelock said. "Just you and me. Let's you and me see if I'm fast enough. The others are out of it."

Bill Chesney was shocked. He had fought his own battles, and he was no coward; but in this he had always thought of the action as a concerted action—of the posse finding this man, executing him, and making an end of it. Or of a gun battle in which all of them took part. None of his thinking had allowed for the chance that suddenly he and this man might come face to face in a shoot-out—just the two of them.

The Key-Lock man was shrewd. He had placed the burden of the fight squarely on Chesney, leaving the others out of it. Nor was there any decent way they could come in if Chesney was killed.

"All right, damn you!" Chesney yelled. "I'll show you for a cheap tin-horn! I'll—"

Behind Matt somebody shouted, and then a smashing blow struck him in the chest. At the same instant his horse reared and he went out of the stirrups and hit the ground hard.

With a frantic eagerness to survive, he scrambled for the crack leading into the canyon. Something was wrong with one of his legs, and his chest felt numb. There was blood on the rocks.

When he reached the crack, he hastily pulled out a handkerchief and packed it tightly over the hole in his chest. Luckily his shirt was snug, and did much to hold the handkerchief in place. He was hurt, but he had no idea how badly.

In the swift instant of action and reaction when he heard that shout, he had seen what had happened. The two men who had pulled off to one side had shot him. He had seen their rifles come up ... but he had seen it too late.

Somebody yelled, "What the hell did you do that for?"

"We came to kill him, didn't we? Well, he's dead," Short answered.

Neill, furious, stared at Short and McAlpin. "That was a dirty—"

He never completed the sentence. From far up the hill, a rifle was talking. He heard the sharp *whap* of a bullet and saw Short go back out of his saddle; and then another shot and McAlpin's horse was buckjumping all over the place.

They scattered for shelter.

Kris lowered her rifle, her calm blue eyes studying the terrain for a target.

"Ma'am," Cooley said, "you better let me take you out of here—"

"Get out," Kris said coldly. "Get away from me."

"Now, you see here!" Cooley grabbed at her bridle rein.

Her rifle was in her hand and she swung the barrel, smashing him across the face. He fell back, lost a stirrup, and struck the ground. As he started to get up, blood flowing from his smashed lip, Kris pointed the muzzle of the rifle at him. Gay Cooley held himself very still. "Look here, ma'am. I didn't mean—"

"Get on your horse and get out. I don't want to see you anywhere around."

"Those men will kill you. You shot at them. They'll kill you, sure."

"Matt's down there," she said, "and I'm going down. You sat there and let them kill him. You saw those men. You knew what they were going to do."

Gay Cooley sat up slowly, putting a hand to his lip. Then he said, "Ma'am, Matt's dead. You saw him go, and those men had him under their guns at short range. You're goin' to need a man, ma'am. Nobody like you can get out of this country alone. I tell you, I—"

She walked her horse around behind him, then suddenly spurred her mount into the brush. Gay lunged to his feet, but she was already out of sight.

He got himself straightened up, and looked carefully around. Keelock's buckskin had run a few feet, then stopped. There was no sign of Keelock's body, nor of any of the other men.

Keelock's pack horses had dashed after Kris, but they were scattered out and running. There was not much chance she would stop for them; and presently they would be scattered over the country from hell to breakfast.

Well, he could round them up himself. There must be quite a lot of grub ... a man could hunt desert country for weeks on what was aboard those pack animals.

He got into the saddle. His lip hurt badly, and he poured water into his palm and bathed his face gent-

ly. That damn' woman! She'd been so quick ... and it
was the last thing he had expected. Who did she
think she was, anyway? And what could she do now,
away to hell and gone back in the mountains like
this?

He glanced down the slope, where Matt's horse
stood fast. Too bad about Keelock ... a good man ...
but a bullet will take the good as well as the bad.

Why couldn't that fool woman see that Matt was
out of it? The dead don't matter.

Gay Cooley had seen a lot of life and of death, and
on the dead he wasted no time. He and Keelock had
always gotten along all right, only this had been
Keelock's fight, not his. He kept telling himself that,
and knew it was true, but it shamed him to think of
it. But the man was dead, and there was no use
letting all that grub go to waste. Nor the woman,
either.

He rode his horse away along the hill toward the
south.

It was past midday, and the afternoon was warm,
sunny, bright. The solitary buzzard had been joined
by a second, and then by a third. A cicada sang in the
brush, a desert wren flipped about among the rocks.
The last echoes of the gunfire had long since died
away. Above the scene, No Man's Mesa loomed ominous and silent, its western shadow thinned to a mere
line.

Far down the hill Neill slowly gathered himself
together and lifted his head warily. He looked up to
where the shots had come from, but there was nothing in sight—there was no movement, no sound.

Suddenly Kimmel was beside him. "Short's hurt ...
he's in bad shape," Kimmel said.

Neill turned himself around and sat down. He removed his hat and ran his fingers back through his
hair. His face was drawn and hard. "We played hell,
Kim. That man was no back-shooter."

"No."

Something scrabbled on the gravel slope, and Chesney appeared. He looked older, and somehow smaller. He glanced at them, his eyes avoiding theirs. "You—you boys all right?"

"Short caught one. Mac's with him."

Chesney looked up. "What in God's name got into them? Why did they shoot?"

"Mac said down to the store at Tuba that the Key-Lock man warned them off him. They figured they had to get him first."

"I could have taken him."

Kimmel looked hard at Chesney. "Bill, you played in luck. That man would have killed you."

"Is he dead?"

"Ain't seen him. But they had him cold."

"He had sand. I was wrong—I took him for a coyote." Chesney straightened up. "We've got to find that woman," he said, "and get her out of here. Only decent thing to do."

Neill glanced at him. It was late to think of doing the decent thing now, but Chesney was right. They must not leave that woman here for Neerland.

"We've got to call off our dog," he said. "We've got to stop Neerland."

Chesney looked blank, then suddenly sounded irritable. "All right, call him off. The job's done, anyway." He started for his horse. "We've got to find that woman and take her out of here—see she gets to safety."

"Maybe she won't want to be found," Kimmel said. "Or she might find us first."

"What's that mean?"

"She was the one that shot Short."

"You're crazy!"

"It's true." Kimmel looked straight at Chesney. "Bill, that woman lifted a rifle and looked right down her sights at Short, and if Mac hadn't hit the dirt he'd have caught one, too."

Chesney led the way down the slope toward the horses of the others. Twice he glanced over his shoulder. Then he drew up. "Maybe that Key-Lock man was just wounded. We'd better find him."

"Leave him alone," Kimmel replied shortly. "If he's alive he'll shoot, and if he lives through this we'll all have to fort up."

When they reached McAlpin he was on his feet, standing over Short. "He'll make it," he said, "but I'd say he cut it thin. If that bullet had been a mite further to the right it would have broken his spine."

He shifted his rifle. "You boys take care of him. I'm goin' after the Key-Lock man."

"Leave him alone," Neill said. "We've done enough."

McAlpin looked around at him. "You do what you've a mind to. I'm goin' to make sure that man's dead. Else he'll be huntin' me ... and all of us."

"We've got to get that woman safe to town," Chesney objected. "We can't leave her out here."

McAlpin's anger was mingled with astonishment. "Damn you, Bill! It was you wanted this man's scalp more than anybody. Now you're pinchin' off the fuse. Why, it was that woman that shot Short an' damn near got me. Look at my horse!"

A livid wound from a grazing bullet lay across the gray's shoulder. "I'll take Short's horse, Bill, and if you're any kind of a man you'll come with me. You got to finish what you started."

"Leave it alone, Bill," Neill advised.

Chesney was torn between quitting a bad job and carrying on with it because of his obligation to finish what he had begun. He started to go, then hesitated. He was sure now—sure ever since the Key-Lock man had offered to face him in open combat—that he had been mistaken. He was positive Johnny Webb had been killed as the Key-Lock man said. Moreover, there was a woman involved; and he had nothing but distaste for the way the man had been shot down while talking it out with Chesney himself. But what McAlpin said was true. He had been the one who built the fire and kept it alive.

"The man's dead, Mac. You saw the way he fell. After all," he said bitterly, "it was you and Short who shot him down."

"Are you callin' me on that?" McAlpin was bitter. "You didn't see him down to Tuba. He told us what would happen if we followed him and by heaven, I believed him then and I do now. If that man lives, no one of us will ever sleep easy again."

Chesney hesitated. Kimmel took his plug from his shirt pocket, examined it carefully, and bit off a small corner. "He's right, Bill," Kimmel said. "We started it. Like it or not, we've got to finish it."

"Count me out," Neill said. "I never liked it. And I like it less now."

"You are out." Chesney's anger at Neill had been growing. He was an upstart. He had no right to be so damned sure of himself. "You're out of everything, as far as I am concerned," Chesney said.

"Of course. That's the way you would be." Neill reined his horse around. "I'll find her and take her back to town if she will come. You do what you've a mind to."

He turned his back on them and rode away, and Kimmel looked after him thoughtfully.

Together, the three men rode to where the buckskin stood. A bullet had hit the saddle horn and glanced off. No doubt it was the shock of this that had made the horse rear. There was blood on the leather of one stirrup, and on the ground where Keelock had fallen.

A thin trail of blood led into the deep crack that split the rim of the canyon. All three eyed the crack with distaste. Only a few feet down the crack took a sharp turn under a shelving ledge. Beyond that point they could see nothing. If anybody wanted to find Keelock they would have to go down into that hole.

They all knew it, and not one of them wanted to do it. Keelock might even have reached the floor of the canyon.

Kimmel walked to the rim and peered over. The canyon was not deep; the floor of it was sand, broken by ledges of rock or fallen boulders or slabs of stone.

He came back to the others. "If he's down there he's well hidden ... All right, I'll go down and have a look."

Nobody spoke up, and he added, "One man can watch this hole—you watch it, Mac." He looked at Chesney. "Bill, you comin', or you goin' to sit this one out?"

"Let's go!" Challenged, Chesney led off, and they rode up the canyon to where the wall was low. Then they rode down.

When they reached the spot below the crack they found blood on the rocks. There was no blood on the sand, but the Key-Lock man had a way of covering his trail. In the deep, loose sand there were too many hoof prints for anything definite to be distinguishable. But they did find one boot track that looked sharp enough to be recent.

Kimmel paused with his hands on his hips. "What d'you think, Bill?"

"He's alive. He's out and away." Chesney was not as positive as he sounded, but it was what he believed most likely. How else could those blood spots have reached the bottom? "Which way do you want to go?" he asked.

Kimmel shrugged. "Makes no difference. Down canyon, I guess." He considered it. "He'll want water. I think he'll go down to Nakia Canyon."

He started down canyon, then drew up. "Bill, Mac's right. We started it—we've got to finish it."

They rode on, watching for tracks or trail sign.

And presently the canyon was empty, and there was no sound, no movement.

twelve

Matt Keelock struggled against the awful blackness, fought against it until his eyes opened slowly ... to more blackness. He lay perfectly still.

Where was he? Was he dead? Had he been buried alive?

The pain was there, so he must be alive. He tried to move and found a new source of agony in his side. He lay still again, eyes wide open. He was looking up into complete darkness.

He lifted a hand. Inches from his face was rock. He lay upon more rock, and rock pressed in upon his side. The searching hand reached out to his right ... nothing. So there was space on his right, space up, out, and down.

Slowly, his thoughts assembled and sorted themselves out. He had been shot. He was in the crevice he had crawled into when he fell. He had passed out there, but not before he had done something ... oh, yes, the blood. He had squeezed blood from his soaked handkerchief on the rocks below, and then he had crawled back in here.

He felt for his six-shooter and found it. Somehow he had gotten the thong over it before he lost it. His bowie knife was there, too.

It was night ... he could smell the coolness of the night air.

Kris ... He must get to Kris. He had told her if anything happened to meet him at that certain place at the base of No Man's Mesa, only a few miles from here. And he knew, knew positively, that if she were alive she would be there ... alive and free, that is.

He had to move, he had to get out of here. They must have searched for him, and if they didn't find him they would return to this place. That was common sense.

Had they left somebody behind? Yes, vaguely he seemed to remember overhearing some talk, remembered the scrape of a boot on rock not far above him.

It was farther to go down than to go up. Besides, he would need a horse, and his buckskin was somewhere on top. As carefully as he could, he lowered his hand and tried to ease the weight of his body off the rock. Little by little he worked his way—soundlessly, he hoped—out of the space beneath the shelf where he lay.

He could see the stars above, the cloudless sky. He smelled smoke.

Somehow he had the impression that one or more of their men had been shot by Kris or Cooley. If so, a wounded man might be close by and might have a fire. That would account for the smoke. His hands and arms were all right. He caught hold of the rocks and lifted himself, feeling his way with infinite care, toward the surface. Before thrusting his head over the top, he listened. Presently he heard a subdued movement that seemed to be some distance away. He permitted himself a careful lifting of his head.

About twenty yards off, was a campfire. He could see the glow of light above it, and the reflection on a man's face, but the fire itself was hidden from his view. He waited, watching ... and considering. If he attempted to crawl out, and the man by the fire turned his head, Keelock would be in full view.

Carefully, he looked about, searching for the horses. He had tried to avoid thinking of his injuries, but his throat was parched and a wetness on his chest told him his wound was bleeding again. Something had happened to his side, perhaps to his hip. It was stiff, and in crawling only the few feet he had so far managed, he had to favor it. Quick movement of any kind was out of the question.

The others, he thought, could not be far off and they would presumably return here, and by daylight they would examine that crevice thoroughly. They might try smoking him out, if the wind was right.

He had no choice, then—he must try to get out now. He could not risk a shot, for a shot might bring the others down on him all the faster.

He held himself there an instant longer, then using his hands and arms, he lifted himself onto the rock. Then, favoring his side, he began to ease himself across the ground.

He was sweating with fear. At any moment the man by the fire might choose to turn his head. Matt Keelock would be in full view for all of thirty or forty yards, although during the last few feet he would be in partial shadow.

The moments dragged with the dragging of his body. A dozen times he felt sure the man must turn, must see him or hear him. His rough clothing rasped lightly against the rocks beneath him, and he could do nothing to prevent it.

Now he was halfway. Using his hands and one knee, he crawled a little farther. A long wedge of shadow showed itself close by, the shadow of a bush or tree, and he veered aside to make for it. He was gasping for breath, and there was a knifing pain in his chest.

The bullet had not touched a lung, or it would have showed in his breathing; and he had not bled as badly as he would have expected. But he had lost a good bit of blood, and it had weakened him.

His hands reached the shadow, then his body. For an instant he rested, and glanced back. The man was standing up, stretching. Now, at last, he turned his head. His face was visible enough for Keelock to recognize him as one of the men from Tuba City. He looked in Keelock's direction, then looked away. He walked around the fire, picking up sticks and breaking them.

He must have been looking into the flames, Keelock thought, and because of that his eyes were almost useless for the darkness.

Matt Keelock lifted himself over a rock, and eased himself through a wall of cedars. Now he was behind the low parapet he had seen just before being shot. He crawled along it, intent only upon distance.

He smelled the horses before he saw them, gathered in a little copse. He crawled nearer, and one of the horses snorted. He swore deep within himself, and then very softly he spoke. "Here, boy! *Here!*"

The horse tugged and the bushes rustled. He crawled nearer, trying to distinguish the animals. The next thing he knew a horse was snuffling at him. He reached up and caught it by the mane and pulled himself up to a standing position. His hand felt the bridle, then his exploring fingers searched for the brand. He was sure this was his horse, by its very manner, but in that darkness he could see hardly at all, for the trees made the night's darkness still deeper. He traced out the brand—it was his own—and then he felt along the bridle to the bushes and, balancing himself by a grip on the mane, he untied the knot with one hand.

By the time he got a grip on the pommel he was so weak he was afraid he might fall. If he did, he would never have the strength to get up again. He hesitated, resting his head against the horse's side.

He took a fresh grip, put the wrong foot in the stirrup and lifted himself to the saddle, sitting down in a side-saddle position. Clinging to the saddle he worked his boot loose from the stirrup and swung his leg across the saddle. Then he spoke very softly to the buckskin and together they walked away into darkness.

Matt made no effort to guide the horse, for it required all his strength just to stay in the saddle, and the buckskin had of his own accord started down hill.

He felt faint and sick, and he leaned far forward, clinging desperately to the pommel. His body lurched with the movements of the horse, and each lurch brought a stab of pain. Yet somehow he stayed in the saddle.

Her first instinct was to get away. Only when she had a mile behind her did she think of the pack animals. She slowed up then and turned in the saddle. They were scattered out behind her, running to catch up . . . at least, some of them were.

She waited until four of them had come up to her, and then started on. They were used to following her horse, and they managed to stay up with her pretty well. There were three more back there, but she was not worried about them. The food and the ammunition, as well as their essential outfits, were carried on the four she now had with her. The question was where to go.

Matt had told her that if they were somehow part-ed to go to the head of the canyon that he believed might offer access to the top of No Man's Mesa. But the men who had hunted him, as well as Gay Cooley, were between her and that rendezvous. She would ride around the mesa.

Matt had showed her the trail up Copper Canyon, and she had only to ride around the south end of No Man's and then go due east to reach that trail. She stopped, dismounted, and ran a lead line to the pack mules, then she rode on.

At sundown she had reached Copper Canyon trail and was starting north. At this very time Matt still lay unconscious in his hiding place.

The night was coming on. A lone star appeared ... a bat swirled above her head, and somewhere far off, a coyote called into the empty desert.

Her rifle was reassuring in her hand, and she held it ready. She was alone now in a vast and empty land, and she rode into uncertainty, with no Matt beside her. The horse alone seemed confident. He was on a trail and it held to the trail.

The walls of the canyon rose on either side. Darkness had closed in, and now it was a relief to look up at the narrow band of sky, with its stars. The night was still.

The tired horse kept on, and the mules followed reluctantly now. None but a tough mountain horse such as she rode could have taken the beating this one had. She herself was exhausted from the long hours in the saddle.

She lost all sense of time. Suddenly the horse lurched, staggered, then lunged upward, scrambling hard on the lip of the cliff. Then a cool night breeze was blowing in her face, and they were out of the canyon.

She paused once to water the horses, to fill the canteens they carried, and to prepare some food for herself. At this place she rested, and for a couple of hours she slept.

When dawn was breaking, she rounded the end of No Man's Mesa and drew up to listen and to study the sand for tracks. Then she rode on.

The mesa curved inward, so that her route led her toward its gigantic wall that lay ahead. Here she was riding with the wall towering above on her left, and she was completely in the shadow.

She went forward with extreme caution, pausing often to listen. At any time she might come upon Gay Cooley, or the party who had attacked them, or Oskar Neerland and those accompanying him. But somewhere ahead was Matt, if he was still alive.

The morning air was still. She was quite sure she could not be seen by anyone unless they were very close, because of the deep shadow of the wall. From what Matt had told her, she recalled that it was all of two miles from the corner ahead to the point at which he believed the mesa might be climbed. There was a notch in the mesa there from which a stream occasionally emerged, but the rest of the time the bed of the stream was dry.

Nervously, she drew her rifle again, brushed a wisp of hair back from her face, and started on. There was no sound but the walking of her horse and the pack animals following, the twittering of birds, and the singing of cicadas out in the sunlight.

Suddenly, she heard a shot. It was far off, but the sound slapped against the cliffs and went echoing off down the wall of rock. Careful to raise no dust, she rode up to the corner. Below her and half a mile away, she saw a wildly running horse, and the saddle was empty.

Her heart pounding, she started forward, standing in the stirrups for a better view. She felt almost sure it was Matt's horse—she would have known him anywhere. But she kept telling herself that she might be mistaken . . . at that distance she could be.

There was dust down there; and then there were

more shots. She was too far away to get there in time
if help was needed, and there would be nothing she
could do. If Matt could escape at all, he would be
escaping to her, coming to her for help, for food, for
ammunition. She went on steadily along the narrow
bench. And then something made her look back.

Three riders!

There had been two men with Oskar Neerland,
Matt believed. Somewhere they had picked up her
trail and they were coming on now behind her. They
might have seen her already, though there was just a
possibility they had not.

The face of the cliff curved back suddenly, and
there in the notch she saw the deep cut of the beginning canyon, and a heavy growth on the far side,
which was only a few yards off. Swiftly she herded
the pack mules into the gap and, grasping her rifle,
she dropped to the ground.

This was where Matt had said he would come; and
this was where she would stay until either he came or
she knew beyond doubt that he was dead.

Within her there seemed to be a vast emptiness, for
every moment of the long ride she had been hoping
against hope that he would be here, that she would
find him waiting for her. Hurt, perhaps, but here.

And now he was not here, nor was there any sign
of him.

It was a good place. Behind her the cliff rose
steeply. In wet weather there was probably a waterfall at this place; now there was a small pool of
water, five or six feet across, a dark, cold pool in a
natural catch-basin.

A trail marked by the hoofs of unshod horses led to
this spot, and someone had placed stones to make a
crude parapet, a defense against attack, or perhaps
against the wind. Behind this she knelt on one knee,
waiting. Beside her on the rock, she placed a row of
cartridges.

Suddenly Neerland came in sight, but a little way off. Without hesitation, she lifted her rifle and put a bullet into the earth right in front of him. His horse leaped and went into a wild fit of bucking. The two men behind him ducked back out of sight.

When the horse quieted, Neerland stared toward where she stood hidden. He was sure enough who it was.

"It's no use, Kris," he said. "You might as well come, give up. I won't leave without you."

She did not reply.

"I know you're there. You come out, or we come after you."

From down on lower ground, among the maze of rocks and broken ground, she heard faint shouts, and then a shot.

Oskar Neerland took out his tobacco and started to build a cigarette. "It's no use," he said again. "They will kill him, if he is not dead already. And if they do not, I shall. You are alone now, unless you come to me."

She realized that he was easing his horse toward her. The horse seemed to be moving restlessly, but somehow each move brought him closer.

She fired again.

Neerland swung his horse quickly, scattering gravel as he leaped back to safety. She had put that bullet within an inch of his skull, the bullet notching his hat brim, and the hat lay there upon the ground to prove it.

She could hear the horse plunging, and she heard Neerland swear, and regretted what trouble she might have caused the horse.

But there was something else ... or had she imagined it?

When that gravel scattered, hadn't there been a sound from below, from down in the gully?

She looked to right and left. With the coming of

night she could not possibly keep them from closing in on her. If they kept to the walls, they might even manage to get behind her.

The mesa rose up on three sides—behind her and to her right and left. She did not dare leave this spot to try to find a way up the cliff, if any way did exist. She waited, listening.

Time passed ... an hour ... two hours ... but nothing happened. The warmth of the sun relaxed her muscles, her lids grew heavy. Several times she changed position. She was very tired, and her head nodded. Then she straightened up, and saw that the distant cliffs were growing brighter with the red glow of the coming sunset.

She realized that she would need all her wits when darkness came. For just a moment she leaned her head against the trunk of a cedar. Then her eyes closed, and she slept.

Over the canyon the buzzards swept in slow, lazy circles. Under the low branches of the cedars the pack mules waited, heads hanging. Kris's horse walked across the open and dipped his muzzle in the cold, still water of the pool.

Matt Keelock had required two hours to stagger and crawl the mile into the canyon. He had remembered the soft sand at the canyon's opening into Nakia, and as his horse raced by it he had kicked his feet loose and, rifle and canteen in hand, had taken a fall into that sand.

Now he was less than a quarter of a mile from the notch in the canyon wall. He was there when the first shot sounded, and when he heard Neerland's voice call out, but he could not distinguish the words. He had heard the second shot not long after that, and then there was silence.

He was dragging one leg, and that pants leg was stiff with blood. However, he doubted if any bones

had been broken. As for his other wound, although
the bullet had gone clear through him, it seemed that
no serious damage had been done to any bone or
vital organ. He knew he was in bad shape, but he had
the iron endurance of a man who has lived a hard life
in a hard country, and he had a choice of moving or
dying. There was no other alternative. The heat in
the canyon was terrific, but the shadow in the lee of
the mesa was not far off.

In the packs that Kris would have there was medi-
cine, there was food ... what he wanted most desperately was a good cup of scalding black coffee. And
there was ammunition. He had done little shooting,
and still had about thirty rounds of rifle and pistol
ammunition.

He managed a hundred yards of fairly easy going,
and pulled and dragged himself up a sixteen-foot dry
waterfall, which luckily was not straight up, but in a
series of three- and four-foot drops. The canteen kept
getting in the way as he crawled, but if he were
pinned down among the rocks it might mean the
difference between life and death. Food he could do
without—he had done it before.

At the top he lay still for a time, panting and trying
to regain some strength. He permitted himself a gulp
of water, holding it in his mouth and allowing a little
at a time to trickle down his throat.

He knew they would have guessed where he was by
now. They would have followed the riderless horse
for some distance, would have discovered the trick,
and would have come back, looking for the place
where he had dropped off. They would have found it
soon enough, but would hesitate to advance rapidly
up a winding canyon where he might be lying in
wait.

Long since he had lost all count of time. He had
fallen down again and again, scrambled up, kept
going. Now it was no longer a matter of will, for it
had become an almost mechanical process.

"*Kris ... Kris, for God's sake, wait for me!*" He whispered the words hoarsely. How many times did he say them?

She had to be there. It was life or death to him now. She had to be there, with the food, the medical supplies. He wanted to live, he wanted desperately to live.

He knew they were back there behind him, and they were good. He had found that out during the day. They were tough men, and they were out to kill him.

He moved on—and fell and lay gasping. Why not just stay right there? What could they do to him that he was not doing to himself? *They can kill you, Matt.* The words came unbidden into his mind. Of course they could kill him, and they would. He started to get up.

In the sand beneath him there were horse tracks ... tracks of unshod horses ... wild horses. How could they have gotten to this place? There must be an easier route that he had missed. And why had they come here?

He pushed himself up, using the rifle, and limped on, staggering at every step, half falling. He crawled up through some boulders and, looking beyond, saw the great split in the wall of No Man's Mesa, seemingly narrow at the top, wider toward the bottom, and several hundred feet high. In another stretch of sand, he found the horse tracks again.

There must be water up there ... that was it. The water in the pool where Kris would be.

He fell down again, and when he started to push himself up, he saw red blood on the sand. The wound had stopped bleeding some time ago, but now it was open again.

Behind him he heard a clattering among the rocks and glanced back, panic-stricken. Something ... somebody was coming.

thirteen

A boot grated in the sand, and Kris woke. She saw the boot, close beside her, and then another boot, and somebody laughed.

"Now ain't that funny? No trouble ... jest none a-tall! She a-layin' there, fell to sleep!"

"Man, that there's a *woman!* Neerland says after he's through with her he'll leave her to us. I say that's mighty nice of him. She's no skinny little whisper of a woman ... this one should *last!*"

She lay perfectly still, in a half-reclining position against the parapet of rocks. *She had failed.* Utterly and completely failed. She had been so careful, she had tried to do everything right. She had found this place and she had arrived in good time. And they had somehow followed her, and then ... then she had fallen asleep.

How many sleepless hours had there been? How many nights before that, of too little sleep? How much bone-weary traveling? She did not really ask these

things of herself, for she sought no excuses. The only
thing now was to find a way out of this.

Her rifle was not beside her . . . they had taken it
from her. Although only two had spoken, she knew
there were three of them. What could she possibly do
against them?

She heard boots strike on stone. Then Oskar Neerland spoke. "No sign of him. He's dead, or he would
have been here."

"*She* ain't."

Neerland looked down at her, and nudged her with
his boot. "Get up. There is no use pretending."

She got up quietly, coolly. She made no protest, no
demand to be let alone. She simply looked from one
to the other. But she was thinking . . . and she found
no help in Muley's face.

The other one, the stocky, thick-set man—now
there might be a possibility. A moment later, feeling
his eyes on her, she was less sure. He was certainly a
tough man, a killer, but she thought he was a man of
temper rather than one with the cold brutality of
Oskar Neerland or the sadistic evil of Muley.

She knew she was in desperate trouble, but she was
thinking clearly. Above all, she must divert them from
any expectation of Matt's arrival, and she must keep
their attention away from the canyon up which he
must come—if he came at all.

"Where is he?" Neerland asked the question as if he
did not really care.

"They killed him. Those other men did. He rode
down to meet them, and two of them were off to one
side. They shot him. I think I killed one of them."

"*You* did?" The heavy-set man showed his surprise.
"How?"

"With this." She indicated the rifle. "I would kill the
other one if I could."

He chuckled, and glanced at Neerland. "We better
watch this one, Oskar."

"I will watch her. Do not worry, Bob."

Neerland walked away a few steps, looking around curiously at the cliffs, and at the brush and trees. The notch at the back where water fell after rains was partly screened by trees and undergrowth, and beyond it a white scar of bared rock could be glimpsed. He merely glanced that way, then walked back.

"If he is dead, why did you come back here?"

"Why?" She seemed astonished. "Why, I mean to find the body and bury it, of course. When those others have gone, I will go down and bury him." She looked Neerland straight in the eyes. "I could not think of him left for the coyotes or buzzards."

"Maybe he is dead ... maybe he is not. We will wait." Neerland watched her. "You will help us to wait."

Her eyes were on the far off valley; there was one small area of open flat down there that was clearly visible. Her eyes were there when the horses came into view, and the golden stallion was leading.

Suddenly her heart began to pound. The wild horses! The faint breeze was from them and toward this place. If nothing turned them aside they would be coming *here!*

What would happen then? Would they turn aside first? Or would they rush into this little area, suddenly find it occupied, and dash away? Would they swirl around in a panic? Or charge on through?

"I was just going to fix something to eat," she said calmly. "Do you mind?"

"All right."

She went to the pack horse and began selecting what she would need. She took her time, wondering how long it would take for the horses to get here, if they were coming. They did come to this place, she knew, for she had seen their tracks, and Matt had told her so.

The men who had been looking for Matt would be down there somewhere, she was thinking; all the more reason for the horses to turn up the canyon.

She left the few things where they were and went about, picking up sticks. Nobody offered to help, and she knew they enjoyed watching her. They were anticipating ... but so was she. Down inside the pack for emergency use was a knife.

She put the sticks together for a fire, then returned to the pack, delaying lighting the fire as long as she could. She put her hand down into the pack and felt the knife hilt. Her own mount was close beside her.

Just then there was a wild shout from down the canyon, and then a thunder of rushing hoofs. She turned swiftly, knife in hand.

She saw the cloud of dust, and suddenly with a burst of inspiration she grasped the pommel and threw herself into the saddle.

Neerland shouted at her, and at that moment the wild horses rushed into the camp. Neerland wheeled and sprang back, stumbling and falling among the rocks. Muley was out of the way, up in the cedars, but Bob was right in the line of the charging horses.

He grabbed wildly for his gun, but another gun rapped a sharp report and Bob, whirling, fell under the pounding hoofs.

Kris, her mount caught in the rush of horses, was swept along. The wild horses, led by the great stallion, plunged through the cedars, straight toward the sheer wall of rock, then swung abruptly around a boulder and rushed up a narrow track. Kris's horse, frightened by the stampede, was running all out, right up the path with the others. He switched back into the trees and she ducked just in time to go under a low branch. Suddenly her horse was scrambling over the rim, and then he was running free. They were atop No Man's Mesa!

Taking a tighter grip on the rein, she swung her horse around.

Matt was there!

He was not only with her, but he was astride the buckskin. Dropping to the ground, she ran to him, and he almost fell from the saddle into her arms. The front of his shirt was covered with blood, and he looked ghastly.

"Rifle," he gasped. "Stop them!"

He clung to the buckskin, and taking the rifle from his hands she ran to the head of the path. She saw no one, but she fired anyway, fired a warning shot to let them know what to expect.

He came to her, walking his horse beside him. He dropped to one knee, the other leg extended, then pulled himself to the rocks.

The wild bunch had scattered away under the trees. The top of the mesa was covered with pine and cedar, and other trees with which she was not familiar. There were open meadows here and there, and from the droppings it was easy to see the horses came here regularly.

One horse, with three white stockings and a scarred hide, had lingered not far away, watching them with pricked up ears. Nothing stirred below.

Kris passed the rifle to Matt, then turned toward the pack animals. All of them, caught in the stampede, had been swept along the trail.

Quickly, she built a fire, starting with dry grass and bits of bark and twigs from the trunks of nearby trees. When the fire was going she put water on to boil; then she unbuttoned Matt's shirt and stripped it off.

The chest wound was inflamed and looked ugly, but she bathed it carefully with warm water. The wound on his hip was less serious, though it was a gash that had cut to the bone. The leg was black and blue from a heavy fall, and the wound looked bad. She started to bathe this too, but he stopped her.

"See that plant?" he said. "The one with the cream-colored flowers? You get some of that, crush it up, and boil it in the water."

"What is it?"

"Cliff rose. It grows all over some of these mesas.

The Hopi wash wounds with it, and it seems to work."

She did as he directed, and noticed that to the westward the great wall of Piute Mesa was bright with sunset colors. In the valley below the shadows were reaching out from No Man's Mesa.

"What will we do?" she asked him later.

"Keep the fire going, then pull back from it." A lightning-struck tree some fifty yards away offered some cover and a good field of fire. "Over there. You let me sleep until trouble comes, or until two hours pass. Then wake me up, and I'll watch, but we've got to keep that fire going. Nobody can top that cliff without showing themselves in the light."

They waited a while, and she reached out for his hand, and held it tightly.

"Old Buck," he said suddenly, "he fell in with the wild bunch and trailed along behind. They were horses, and they were company, and he may have figured we had stayed close to them before, so there must be a reason.

"I was all in ... I couldn't have made it another foot. You should have seen him when he found me ... like a playful pup. It was all I could do to get up on him."

"Will they try to come up here, Matt?"

"Kris ... you watch. I ..." His words trailed off into a mumble, and he was asleep.

The sun had gone. Far away across the desert land the sandstone ridges and cliffs still held the sun's fire, but here on the mesa the light was a dusty lemon. Under the trees it was shadowed and still. She went to the mules and loosened their packs, letting them fall; then she removed the saddles. The grateful animals rolled in the grass, shook themselves, and rolled again. Keeping a careful eye on the head of the trail, she unsaddled the horses and picketed them on the grass.

It was very quiet. She carried several armloads of fuel to the fire and placed it within easy reach.

Around the lightning-blasted tree there was a good
bit of fuel—broken limbs, dried and seasoned, as well
as a good-sized piece of the tree itself that had broken off and fallen to the ground.

The horse with the three white stockings showed
no disposition to leave them. This was an old horse,
and some nostalgic memory of campfires and the man
smell kept it close to them. Running with the wild
bunch was probably growing increasingly difficult.

She checked his rifle, reloading the fired cartridges,
and checked her own. She got his pistol and reloaded
the empty chambers. She was somewhat frightened of
what might come, and yet it was not really fear.
Injured he might be, but this was her man, and
where he was there could be no real fear.

The sky became a deep, dark blue; the first stars
came out. The nearby ridges were black, mysterious.
The coolness of night had come, and it felt good. She
got a ground sheet from the packs and ever so gently
drew Matt onto it; then she got a blanket and covered him.

She was restless, and walked away from the fire to
the dark edge of the cliff to listen. There was a fire
down there.

Her eyes moved off toward the south, remembering
the great, silent cave houses where they had stayed,
and where she had so hopefully planted a garden. . . .

They would come tonight, she was sure they
would. And when they came, she would be ready.

fourteen

Neill rode into Freedom with Short tied over a saddle.

Somebody shouted, and people came out into the street. Sam, drying his hands on his apron, emerged from the saloon just behind Hardin and John Ware. Taplinger was there, too, and George Benson.

Neill drew up. "Yes, it's Short. He's dead, and we've played hell. If we don't stop them, they'll murder that man Keelock, and his wife, too."

"Wife?"

"She's with him. In fact," he added grimly, "she was the one who killed Short. Keelock was talking to Chesney, and it looked as if they were going to settle it between them, and then McAlpin and Short cut loose and shot Keelock out of the saddle."

"They didn't kill him?"

"Not by a long shot! But if we don't get back in there and stop them, they will; and if they do, they will have to kill her."

Neill saw Taplinger then, and his fury mounted. "Yes, and that damned marshal you hired is in there with two murdering thieves."

Taplinger's face flushed, and he started to protest, but Neill broke in. "You'd no right to hire that legal murderer and give him a right to kill a man and his wife." His tone was harsh, and his voice carried a new authority.

"Now, see here!" Taplinger began. "I—"

Neill turned his back on him. "Hardin," he said quickly, "if you'll come with me, we'll go back in there and stop this. If they kill those two it will be a disgrace this community will never live down."

"Tell me just what has happened," Ware said. "I've heard little about it."

Neill dismounted and Taplinger started forward, but Neill pointedly ignored him and went into the saloon, followed by Ware and Hardin. As briefly as possible he outlined the trouble from the beginning. Finally he said, "By the time we get back it may be too late, but I could do nothing alone short of killing some of them myself."

Hardin studied Neill thoughtfully. After a moment he said, "You've changed, boy. This business has changed you."

"Maybe ... and maybe that's why I spoke out against it. And while I tried to get Short back here alive, I thought more and more about it. We've got to get back in there and stop this."

"Do they still believe Keelock murdered Johnny Webb?" Hardin asked.

"No, and that's the worst of it. They know he didn't, but they are still trying to kill him. Partly because they are afraid of what will happen if they don't."

"What about this man Neerland?" Ware asked.

"That's a grudge affair. What Neerland may have in mind, I don't know or care, but he simply wanted a legal cloak to cover him while he committed murder. The man's far from a fool, and he's dangerous."

"What about Mrs. Keelock?"

"Skin told me at Tuba that she was a lady, every inch of her. We were for getting her out of there. At least Bill and I were for it—yes, and Kimmel, too, I think. I looked for her, I didn't find her."

"All right," Hardin said, "we'll ride back in there and put a stop to it." And Ware agreed. "You're right, Neill. It must be stopped."

Nine men rode out of Freedom, nine men with just one idea, to reach the scene before their community could be branded for murder. They left in the cool of the evening and they rode fast, changing horses twice before they reached Tuba City.

Neill, hoping and expecting that the men of Freedom would be with him, had arranged for horses to be waiting for them at Tuba. Yet swiftly as they rode, he knew there was hardly one chance in a thousand that they would arrive in time.

But he was banking on the courage of the man Keelock, and of a woman whom he had never met.

Two hours had passed, but she did not wake Matt. He was resting easily for the first time since he was wounded. He did not even wake when she gently changed the dressing on his chest, using more of the crushed cliff rose. He muttered in his sleep, but slept on.

Twice she added fuel to the fire near the cliff edge, approaching it with care, and each time she listened from the dark rim beyond the range of the firelight, but she heard no sound.

The night wore on, and her weariness grew. It was long past midnight when she at last knew she could wait no longer. If she fell asleep again, as she had when on watch below the cliff, it would be the end— they would be killed in their sleep. She dared not chance it. She went to Matt and touched his shoulder. "Matt? Matt, wake up."

He stirred under her hand, then his eyes flared open. When he sat up, she went to the fire and filled a cup with coffee. A soft wind stirred the fire, bending the long flames.

He took the coffee, and when she looked down at him as he sat there on the ground she was shocked by the gauntness of his features. But when he had finished the coffee, he got up by himself.

The wind guttered the fire again, and off in the distance thunder rolled. Matt turned his head around sharply. A great bank of black clouds had rolled up; and even as he looked, a streak of jagged lightning struck a distant ridge and made a vivid, momentary fringe of light along the crest.

He caught up the rifle. "We've got to get the horses in and keep them close," he said. A few spattering drops of rain fell. "This will put out our fire."

Limping to the buckskin, he led the animal close, and then on a sudden inspiration he picked up the saddle and threw it on the horse's back. Swiftly he tightened the cinch and slipped on the bridle. Then he saddled Kris's horse. When she brought the pack animals in, he strapped on the pack saddles and loaded up.

He heaped more fuel on the fire, and then pulled himself into the saddle and they started north along the mesa. Moving over close to her he leaned nearer and said, "From down below I saw some rough, broken country about a mile north of here. We might find some shelter there." And he added, "There's less chance of getting struck by lightning on lower ground."

The few spatters of rain had turned into a quick downpour, but both of them had donned slickers, and they rode on in the rain, the mules on a lead rope.

In the light of the lightning flashes, they found a place where the surface rock broke off, and descended almost two hundred feet by an easy route. To the east they could see where the break was sharper, and turned that way to get under the lee of the escarpment.

Once there, they found another descent and went lower still to a place where the ledge of rock had been undercut by water and wind to make a deep shelter.

The rain ceased, and in the quiet that followed they secured the horses under the shelter, and the mules beside them. Then they stripped off the packs and saddles. Kris was just shaking out a bed for them when the rain came again.

It came with a roar. The sky was weirdly lit by lightning, and the thunder crashed and rolled. Sure that they would never be found in such a storm, they drew together for warmth and lay staring into the wild night. And lying so, they slept.

Chesney, Kimmel, and McAlpin came up to the camp at the foot of No Man's Mesa in the bright sunlight of the morning after the rain. They had waited out the flash flood that filled the canyon with a rushing river, and when it had run its way on into the desert and the natural catch-basins below, they rode up on the hard-packed sand.

There was no pleasure in Oskar Neerland's eyes when they appeared, and even less in those of Muley when he saw Gay Cooley was riding with them.

"They got away?" Chesney asked, almost hoping they had.

"Up there." Neerland jerked a thumb toward the mesa's rim.

"You mean there's a way up?" It was Cooley who spoke. His eyes went to Muley's, then he looked around him very carefully. It was hard to tell what he was thinking.

"They found a way," Muley said. "Followed some broomtails, an' they went right up."

"You haven't been up there?"

"They had a fire going right on the rim until the rain put it out. It has not been lighted again, so they must have gone."

Kimmel interrupted. "I thought there was three of you."

"Bob Mitchell's dead. Matt Keelock shot him, then the horses ran over him. We dragged him over yonder."

They looked in that direction, but did not ride over. Bob Mitchell had been known to them as a hard character and a dangerous one. The country, they felt, was better off without him.

"All right," Chesney said, "let's go get them."

Neerland did not move. "You have given the job to me," he said. "I will do it."

"We're all here," Chesney said. "We might as well help."

"I shall need no help."

"There's a woman up there," Chesney said, "who had no part in the killing of Johnny Webb. We want to take her back to town."

"I will take care of the woman."

For the first time in many years Chesney was unsure of himself. Oskar Neerland was a dangerous man, but he did not fear him. The trouble was, he himself had been one of those who appointed this man the marshal. He himself had directed him to hunt down Matt Keelock.

"That woman must be protected," he objected now. "We will see that she gets back to Freedom and the stage line."

"I will take care of her, and I do not want your help. Go away."

"To hell with her!" McAlpin exclaimed. "She killed Short. She tried to kill me."

"We're riding along, Neerland," Chesney said. "We want to see that woman is safe."

"I am the law." Neerland spoke in a flat tone. "If you interfere, I shall arrest you."

"I don't think so," Kimmel said.

"You're fired, Neerland," Chesney said. "You ride back to Freedom."

Neerland did not even smile. He was contemptuous. "You cannot discharge me. You do not have the votes. I know your rule of voting."

Muley had drawn off to one side, and Chesney was aware that he had a corner on them. But he was not going to back down now.

"Count me out," McAlpin said. "I don't care what happens to her."

"Why argue?" Muley said. "There's enough woman there for all of us."

Chesney's face showed his shock. "By—" he began, but Kimmel's cool voice interrupted. "Forget it, Bill. She's no affair of ours. Let's get out of here."

"Kim, why you—!"

"Bill, *let's get out of here!*"

Kimmel's tone brought a breath of sanity to Chesney's anger. He turned to Kimmel and saw his eyes, saw the warning in them.

He took a quick grip on himself. "Oh, the hell with it!" he said, and they rode away.

When they had gone no more than fifty yards, he turned on Kimmel. "If you think I'm—"

"Shut up, Bill. They can still hear you." Kimmel's low tone was persuasive. "Why get yourself killed and do no good? That other fellow had him a shotgun."

"If you think I'm afraid, you've got another think coming!"

"You ain't scared," Kimmel said, "you're just a damn' bull-headed fool. You get an idea crossways in your skull and nothin' in God's world can get past it. All we've got to do is let them go on up, then follow them. It's simple as that."

Chesney felt like a fool. Of course. Anybody should have realized that, and there he was, about to walk bull-headed into a shotgun.

"Where's Cooley?" he asked, suddenly thinking of him.

"He stayed back there, with them."

McAlpin had not stayed behind. He rode with them, but neither man looked at him or recognized his presence. Angered by being ignored, he broke in. "If you think I'm goin' back up there, you're crazy!"

Kimmel looked around at him. "Mac, we had no idea you'd go along, and if you'll take my advice you'll go back to Freedom, you'll sell those scrubs of yours to whoever will buy 'em, and you'll pull out. I don't care where you go, but I've got an idea you aren't goin' to like it around Freedom any more."

They walked their horses away and left him sitting there staring after them. Short was gone and nobody was talking about the Lost Wagons any more, and of a sudden he realized what Kimmel had said was true. He was not going to like it around Freedom after this.

"Kim," Chesney said, "I've played the fool. All I could think of was Johnny dead and some rawhider had shot him in the back. I was crazy to hang that Key-Lock man."

"You weren't alone."

"I was the worst. I was drivin' after it. That was why Hardin pulled out. And Neill."

"They're good men, Bill."

Chesney gathered his reins. "All right, Kim, let's ride back and get that woman out of there, anyway."

He was silent for several minutes. "I don't like it, Kim—that Neerland going after that man."

"You leave 'em alone," Kim replied calmly. "That Key-Lock man is an old lobo. He's from away back at the forks of the crick. Anybody who gets that man in a corner has bit off a chunk, believe me, and he'd better have the jaws to chew it!"

The camp was empty when they reached it, but

the tracks showed them the trail up the mountain. It was tucked away behind a thick clump of cedars, and there was no indication of a trail until you got right to it. Hidden below by the thick growth and by broken rock, it led up steeply.

At the top they found themselves standing with all the world spread out around them.

"We've got to find that woman, Kim," Chesney said urgently. "Else something will happen here that will bring us shame to our last days."

Kimmel's horse switched his tail restlessly. The rain had destroyed the tracks. If they chose the wrong way, they might easily arrive too late.

And then they heard a shot.

fifteen

Matt Keelock woke with the first light. He clasped his hands behind his head. For the first time in days he was thinking really clearly. Tentatively, he moved his leg. The wound on his hip had never been much more than an annoyance, but the fall had made his leg one great bruise from hip to knee. This morning it felt better.

He eased from under the blankets and pulled on his boots. Then he put on his gun belt, took out his Colt, and spun the cylinder.

From the overhang, he looked out over what was in essence a hanging valley, approximately a mile long and, at the head where their camp was, not over a quarter of a mile wide. It was green and beautiful under the warm morning sun, fresh after the fall of rain.

He went to the horses, checked their hoofs, and looked them over generally. The mules seemed cheer-

ful enough, and he released them to wander down on
the rich grass not far away.

Then he went back to their shelter, where he
looked down at Kris. Her face looked tranquil and
unbelievably lovely in repose. He hesitated to wake
her, knowing what was to come. He knew too much
about the sort of men who pursued him not to realize
that it would all be over, one way or another, before
this day was past.

They would be coming soon. It would take them a
while to locate him, and much as he wanted a cup of
coffee, he was not going to make it easy for them by
lighting a fire and lifting a smoke.

He went to one of the packs and got out a thick
wad of rawhide strips that he had planned to use in
plaiting a riata. He tied several of them end to end,
then walked to a boulder some fifty feet away, found
a chunk of rock of the right size, and made a four-
way wrap-around tie. Then he trailed the rawhide
along the ground under the grass and dust, to the
overhang.

After that he dug around in his gear and found a
can of peaches, which he opened. With his Winchester close by, he sat down on a rock and began eating
them. He speared each half, cut it in half, and lifted it
to his mouth with the point of his knife. When he had
eaten the peaches he drank the juice.

He heard Kris stirring in the blankets, and was
about to turn when he saw one of the mules look up
suddenly. He got to his feet.

"What is it, Matt?" Kris said.

Without turning his head, he replied, "What we've
been expecting, Kris. I think we'll make an end to it
here."

"What can I do?"

"When I say, 'Jim, don't shoot,' you pull on that
string. Pull good and hard."

"Is that all?" she asked, and he nodded.

Three riders had stopped on the rim above them.

He knew there were three, because they had the sunrise at their backs and their shadows fell on the wall opposite.

Three?

He had seen Bob Mitchell go down before his gun, had seen some of the stampede sweep over him. Who, then, was the third?

"Stay out of this," he said softly to Kris. "I do not want to think of you now."

"All right," she said. And then she added, "Here they come."

He could see them working their way down the slope at almost the place where he and Kris had descended. They were a good three hundred yards off, and he might have taken one of them out, but he was not sure who they were, nor did he want to turn this into a sniping operation. He wanted to see them face to face, and win or lose that way.

When they were almost abreast of the overhang, he stepped into view. On his left was a thick cedar, gnarled and ancient. On his right a broken slab from one of the ledges above.

"You came a long way for it."

They brought up short, and he said casually, "You've played the fool, Gay. You've wasted your life hunting that gold."

"Like hell! It's here. We've found it."

"You mean you've swapped it for a belly full of lead."

Muley had the shotgun, and that shotgun worried him. At the distance it was a dangerous weapon. But he had given it thought. And Muley had an instinct for survival.

Oskar Neerland was kooking for Kris, and she was not in sight. His eyes returned to Matt. The sneer his face always wore was deeper now.

"You have to die," he said. "I promised it. I promised myself to kill you, and then to take the woman."

He was going to draw. Matt saw it clearly, and he shouted, "Jim, don't shoot!"

Something crashed in the brush and Muley pivoted, his shotgun lifted toward the brush.

Neerland drew, and Matt stepped forward and down. He had planned it nicely, believing Neerland to be a dead shot, and hoping for it. A wild shot might have wasted his strategy, for the foward step took him two feet down. He had studied that spot, planned for it; and when his foot landed, he fired.

And missed!

Neerland's bullet had whipped by over his head, but now the gun muzzle lowered, and Matt went forward and down another step, and then he fired once more. A bullet whipped by near him. He was thinking that would be Cooley, and then he fired and fired again.

A shot spattered bark into his face, half blinding him, and he let himself fall forward onto one knee. His left forearm came up, his gun barrel lay across it, and he fired again. Fired into the widening crimson blot on the front of Neerland's shirt. He saw the big man start to fall, and he swung his gun to Cooley, who traded shots with him. Both men missed, and then Matt lunged to his feet and fired again.

The bullet knocked Cooley sidewise in the saddle and he yelled, *"I quit!"*

"The hell you do!" Matt fired again, and Cooley fell off his horse.

A rifle roared, then another. Muley brought his shotgun to bear at last, but he dropped it and slapped the spurs to his horse. Another shot, and he was racing like a madman down the valley with bullets dusting him at every step.

On the rim were half a dozen riders, all with rifles, but there was no scoring a hit at the distance. The horse, stung perhaps, and frantic with fear, was now a runaway.

He was still running when he reached the rim. They

all saw it clearly enough. The maddened animal took one enormous leap out into space, seemed to hang suspended for an instant, then dropped from sight. At that point there was a drop of five hundred feet.

The riders from the rim above were coming down.

Matt Keelock walked forward and stood over Neerland. The man was alive, his eyes fastening on Matt in a fixed and awful stare. But he was dying, dying hard and slow.

"You came of your own will," Matt said, "I had no strings on you."

Deliberately, he turned away, and went over to Cooley. He held his gun ready, but there was no fight in the man.

"It was the Lost Wagons," Cooley said. "That gold ruined me. Right from the day we left California."

"You did all that killing?"

"Me? No, that was Muley. We thought he was just a youngster we were helpin' out. Instead, he figured from the first day that he'd kill us all."

"When did you find out?"

Gay Cooley threw him a guilty look. "That was the worst of it. When the second man died, I was pretty sure."

Matt looked down at him, reflecting at the curious turn things could take. There were two bullets in him, but he was going to make it. Right now this man was in better shape than he was himself. He backed up a step and sat down, careful to keep his gun up.

Kris was talking to the men who came off the rim. They were all approaching now; he could hear their voices.

"It was those Lost Wagons," Cooley said. "I was a pretty good man until then. Muley, he wanted all that gold for himself, and I was just as bad."

"Cooley wasn't your name?"

"It was Hollenbeck ... Ben Hollenbeck. I dropped out of sight and let everybody think we were all dead. The trouble was, all this country looks alike after a few years, and I'd have taken oath that gold was seven or eight miles south of here. That much, at least.

"I figured I could come right back to it, but the way things worked out, it was a couple of years. The worst of it was, when I went out of this piece of country I never took time to look back, and it all looks different coming at it from the south.

"Four or five times I knew I was within a short distance of it, but every time I turned south. I couldn't believe we had come north any further.

"Then I saw that place at the foot of the mesa. That was where Muley was left, all tied up, and I recognized it on sight. I knew it was the place, but it still didn't look right."

"Did you ever think that Valadon deliberately wrote his directions wrong?" Matt said. "You could have been influenced by that."

The men had all ridden up now, and he knew four of the faces as those of men who had hunted him. The others were strangers.

Neill swung down. "Keelock, I'm Neill, and I'm sorry. We had the wrong idea about you."

"It was me," Chesney said. "I ramrodded the whole thing. I figured you for a yellow back-shooter and I wouldn't listen to anything else. I was wrong."

"It was a fair shooting," Matt said quietly.

"I know, and I played hell."

Matt turned away, resting a hand on Kris's shoulder. "I've got to lie down, Kris." He looked back at the men and gestured toward Cooley. "You do whatever you've a mind to with him. He won't be looking for the Lost Wagons any more."

Cooley twisted toward him. "Why is that?"

"Because I found 'em." Matt took a wagon-bolt from his belt. "Ever see that before, Cooley? It was your marker, stuck into a crack in the rock wall."

His hand on Kris's shoulder, he limped to their

shelter. When he reached it, he almost fell onto the bed.

"In a couple of days we'll ride out of here, Kris."

"What about the stallion?"

"We'll come back for him."

He stretched out, easing his bruised leg to its full length. "Kris," he said, "make some coffee, will you? I'm tired."

ABOUT THE AUTHOR

"I think of myself in the oral tradition—as a troubadour, a village taleteller, the man in the shadows of the campfire. That's the way I'd like to be remembered—as a storyteller. A good storyteller."

It is doubtful that any author could be as at home in the world recreated in his novels as Louis Dearborn L'Amour. Not only could he physically fill the boots of the rugged characters he writes about, but he has literally "walked the land my characters walk." His personal experiences as well as his lifelong devotion to historical research have combined to give Mr. L'Amour the unique knowledge and understanding of the people, events, and challenge of the American frontier that have become the hallmarks of his popularity.

Of French-Irish descent, Mr. L'Amour can trace his own family in North America back to the early 1600s and follow their steady progression westward, "always on the frontier." As a boy growing up in Jamestown, North Dakota, he absorbed all he could about his family's frontier heritage, including the story of his great-grandfather who was scalped by Sioux warriors.

Spurred by an eager curiosity and desire to broaden his horizons, Mr. L'Amour left home at the age of fifteen and enjoyed a wide variety of jobs including seaman, lumberjack, elephant handler, skinner of dead cattle, assessment miner, and officer on tank destroyers during World War II. During his "yondering" days he also circled the world on a freighter, sailed a dhow on the Red Sea, was shipwrecked in the West Indies and stranded in the Mojave Desert. He has won fifty-one of fifty-nine fights as a professional boxer and worked as a journalist and lecturer. A voracious reader and collector of rare books, Mr. L'Amour's personal library of some 10,000 volumes covers a broad range of scholarly disciplines including many personal papers, maps, and diaries of the pioneers.

Mr. L'Amour "wanted to write almost from the time I could walk." After developing a widespread following for his many adventure stories written for the fiction magazines, Mr. L'Amour published his first full-length novel, *Hondo*, in 1953. Mr. L'Amour is now one of the four bestselling living novelists in the world. Every one of his more than 85 novels is constantly in print and every one has sold more than one million copies, giving him more million-copy bestsellers than any other living author. His books have been translated into more than a dozen languages, and more than thirty of his novels and stories have been made into feature films and television movies.

Among Mr. L'Amour's most popular books are *The Lonesome Gods, Comstock Lode, The Cherokee Trail, Flint, Son of a Wanted Man, The Shadow Riders, Silver Canyon, Bowdrie, The Walking Drum*, his historical novel of the 12th century, and his series of novels which tells the continuing saga of the Sackett family, the latest of which is the bestseller *Jubal Sackett*.

The recipient of many great honors and awards, in 1983 Mr. L'Amour became the first novelist ever to be awarded a Special National Gold Medal by the United States Congress in honor of his life's work. In 1984 he was also awarded the Medal of Freedom by President Ronald Reagan.

Mr. L'Amour lives in Los Angeles with his wife, Kathy, and their two children, Beau and Angelique.